Valiant, He Endured

17 Sci-Fi Myths of Insolent Grit

George Donnelly, Editor

THERE WILL BE LIBERTY NO. 2

Want Book 3 Free?

If you liked *Valiant, He Endured*, you'll LOVE *Intrepid, She Blasted*, the third book in the *There Will Be Liberty* anthology series, due out April 2017.

VISIT THE LINK AND
CLAIM YOUR EBOOK, FREE.

GeorgeDonnelly.com/ISB

Thank you for reading!

For a voluntary world

Contents

Unwholesome Victuals
by Michael DiBaggio

Jonathan awoke with a startled gasp that erupted into a violent coughing fit. He instinctively reached for the rag at his bedside, stained with flecks of blood and sputum, and clamped it over his mouth.

When the spell finally passed and he drew breath again, he turned gingerly to his side, his whole body quaking, and addressed the man standing next to him. "Is it morning already, James?"

In the early morning darkness and his confused state of exhaustion, Jonathan did not notice that the man with a kerosene lantern in hand and attired in dark blue fatigues and khaki suspenders was not his usual orderly. Nor did Jonathan make any comment about the short wooden pole the man wielded, though he thought it an unusually rough method of rousing.

Even bedridden in the hospital, Jonathan was the perpetually cheerful and generous sort. He was a born believer in the goodness of other men, and an optimist in the bargain. When his physician diagnosed him with consumption, Jonathan wasted no energy in despair, and he placed the utmost confidence in Dr. Barret's assurances that, with the aid of "clean, cool air and wholesome victuals" he would make a full recovery.

Not even the surprise of the Invasion and the unbroken chain of enemy victories were able to darken his sunny outlook. When the first advance of the Tripods was thrown back at Aberdeen, Jonathan said to his fellows in the sick ward, "See, gentlemen? Just as I have said." When further assaults brought the enemy closer to Baltimore, and finally laid the city under siege, Jonathan's indefatigable optimism was a source of great encouragement to those around him. He was not daunted by the restrictive rationing or the increasing cruelties that the Federal soldiers inflicted on the populace. He could speak of electricity and soap without becoming bitter at their lack, and gnaw horse meat while recalling fond memories of salted pork and fresh apples. When rumor spread that the invaders had filled the harbor with a mat of red weeds so tangled and thick that even the mighty screws of the battleship *Massachusetts* were fouled, Jonathan consoled his fellows with his firm conviction that the siege would soon be lifted by the long-rumored relief force. And when news arrived that said relief force had been annihilated in the Cumberland Gap, he was not downcast for more than a few minutes.

At that point, Jonathan's obstinacy in the face of grim reality became a source of vexation rather than encouragement. Many of his caregivers and fellow patients grew to hate him. He returned their mocking only with goodwill and further optimism. When others trembled in dread of some strange, far-off cacophony, he assured them that it was the roar of one of the Gun Club's great bombards, the engines of Frank Reade's aerial battleships, or some other wonder weapon certain to bring them victory.

And so, having a stick jammed into his ribs was hardly enough to perturb Jonathan.

"I ain't James." The curt speech of the prodding stranger was muffled by the scarf tied over his lips. "Can you walk?"

Jonathan favored him with a wan smile. "Why yes, yes I believe I can, today. If I can just lean on you, and we start very slowly—"

The soldier snapped his head to the side impatiently, yelling, "Bring a litter!" He stormed away without further conversation.

As several more soldiers rolled Jonathan off his cot into the litter, he could hear the first man's voice echoing down the darkened hallway, repeating that question to the other patients. The corridors were filled with other uniformed men, some with slung rifles, all of them masked, carrying laden stretchers.

As they were carrying Jonathan down the stairwell, he politely asked about the unusual circumstances. One of the soldiers, a much friendlier chap than the one who woke him, spoke reassuringly.

"A hole's opened up in the enemy lines. We're evacuating the sick first. You'll be taken out of the city to receive better care."

"Thank God!" Jonathan exclaimed, and silently he thought, 'See, gentlemen? Just as I have said.'

The two soldiers deposited him in the hospital courtyard and helped him off the litter and onto the grass.

"The wagons are all loaded up now, but they'll be back. Stay here until they call you," the friendly soldier said. "And good luck to you!"

Indeed, several horse-drawn wagons were already clopping off through the gate, and the last remaining wagon, burdened with patients, was being waved off by other soldiers. A handful of consumptives were left with Jonathan, many of them moaning of their treatment in between hacking fits.

"Oh, God, the chill! Do they mean to kill us, casting us out in the cold air like this?" one asked. Jonathan realized that not all of the patients had heard the happy news, and he hurried to tell them.

"Shut up!" one of them barked.

"We've heard just about enough of your fantasies," rejoined another.

Jonathan didn't bother to correct them again. The cold October wind was blowing from the north; it bit into his frail frame through the thin fabric of his nightclothes, and he hugged himself as he shivered. He cleared his mind of all thoughts but the joyful news, and he remembered that Dr. Barret had told him the value of clean, cold air. He took in a deep breath through his open mouth, but his throat stung and his lungs burned like fire, and he burst into another coughing spell.

When he finally recovered, Jonathan's ringing ears perceived the voice of Dr. Barret. He craned his neck, searching the courtyard for him, eager that the kindly physician should find his way over to deliver the happy news and vindicate Jonathan's faith.

Instead, he spied the doctor's tall and spare figure vehemently arguing with a group of soldiers. The doctor looked like he had been roused from bed as abruptly and thoughtlessly as Jonathan was, for he was dressed very hastily in a half-buttoned jacket and a crooked cravat and his wispy hair blew in the wind. Jonathan found the usually immaculate doctor's disheveled appearance concerning. The physician was very animated, and his words soon turned into shouting, loud enough for the entire courtyard to hear.

"Where is Colonel Huntsinger? These men are not fit to be turned out of bed! You will not remove one more of them until I have spoken to Colonel Huntsinger! Where is he?"

"Colonel Huntsinger has been relieved for dereliction of duty, a fate that you are largely responsible for, Dr. Barret," replied one of the soldiers. The pistol on his hip and the decoration on his heavy wool coat identified him as an officer. "I've taken his place as chief physician, so anything you wanted to say to him you can say to me."

"These are my patients! They are human beings! They are not the Army's to dispose of!"

"General Order 29, which you have been defying for weeks, says otherwise: 'No one stricken with communicable disease shall be harbored within the city.' Here is a copy of the order so that you can adhere to it more closely in the future." The officer produced a sheet of paper and handed it to the doctor, who promptly tore it up.

"Your orders can go to hell, and General Otis along with them! He is a fiend and a devil, spawned from the same black pit as the invaders! Do you think I don't know what you're really doing? Do you think I don't know where you're taking—"

Dr. Barret was interrupted by his own sharp cry of pain. One of the other soldiers rammed the butt of his rifle into the doctor's stomach, and another followed with a blow between his shoulder blades. Dr. Barret collapsed amid a scramble of kicking legs and descending cudgels.

Jonathan recoiled and fell backward onto the grass. He convulsed with another agonizing, raking cough and found that for the first time in many weeks, he could not suppress his doubt and fear.

***

The cold, gray light of dawn was just beginning to filter over the horizon as Jonathan's wagon rolled through the gate at the first ring of earthworks that encircled the city. The road was loosely compacted dirt, crisscrossed with ruts and half washed out, and the wagon pitched and jolted its wretched passengers with bone-shaking force. Jonathan took measured breaths, hoping not to excite another coughing spell. In the miserable hour he spent shivering waiting for the wagon, he had given up the idea that cold air was a help to his condition.

The convoy wended toward the northeast, passing beside and underneath the line of fortifications. Jonathan half-expected to see the lines deserted, and a swell of infantry moving alongside them to recapture the farther perimeter, but sheltering troops still crowded beneath the high berms, cooking their meager breakfasts. He could see men with field glasses leaning out of the armored watchtowers that rose up from behind the trenches, and bored artillerymen leaning on the open breeches of their guns or playing cards behind the barbettes. The soldiers, including the pair that rode in the wagon with the sick, seemed peculiarly subdued, and yet they must have known about the break in the Martian line. Perhaps, thought Jonathan, a sortie had already been launched, and the men on the lines were merely the reserves.

A loud droning sound broke from the east, and the soldiers on the lines all turned to look in its direction. A chorus of similar sounds backed up the first, followed by the clank and clatter of artillery mechanisms and the confused shouting of men. The teamsters urged the horses on, snapping the reins furiously, and the wagon convoy soon left the fortifications behind.

Eventually, they slowed amid a moonscape of mud-bottomed craters and crumbled casemates littered with warped gun barrels, empty shell casings, and charred helmets. The droning noise kicked up again, closer this time. Jonathan heard one of the teamsters yell, "That's far enough!" and he brought the wagon to a halt.

Immediately, one of their escorts leaped off the back of

the wagon and unlatched the tailgate while the other soldier rammed the butt of his rifle into the backs of the sick passengers, forcing them out. "Everybody out! Shake a leg, god damn you!"

Jonathan began to protest, but the press of bodies turned him around and forced him back, and he tumbled to the wet dirt. All around him were dozens of people—men and women, children and elderly—many he knew from the hospital, but others he had never seen. All of them appeared sick or somehow injured, many of them seriously. The soldiers liberally donated their boot heels and rifle butts to this storehouse of woes.

As the violence increased and a few of the wagons dashed away, the tumult of confused and angry voices gave way to a choir of screams and desperate pleading. Old men with palsied hands struggled in vain to pull themselves back aboard the wagons. Fever-stricken children grabbed at the pants of passing soldiers, crying deliriously for their mothers. Frail women collapsed to the mud on their knees, their hands clasped in supplication either to the soldiers or to God. One cry was universal: "Do not abandon us! Do not leave us to die!"

The effect of this pitiful scene was soon evident, as several of the soldiers, their hearts not behind their dreadful duties, added their own mournful sobs and pleas for forgiveness. One man knelt down, tore off his scarf and embraced the ill, determined to share their fate. Another halted his staggering steps just before reaching the wagon and turned to look at the huddled masses of the abandoned sick. Overcome with grief, he unholstered his revolver and shot himself in the temple.

Those with less remorse ran to the wagons under the urgent imprecations of the teamsters, trampling any who blocked their way. With supreme effort of strength, Jonathan surged to his feet and caught one of the retreating soldiers by the collar and held on despite the blows of his fists.

"Why? In the name of God, why?" he demanded. But his grip soon faltered, and he was cast to the ground without receiving an answer.

Mired in the filth, Jonathan surrendered to the weakness and exhaustion in his cold-numbed limbs. His last quanta of hope and faith in the virtue of men drained with his tears into the mud.

"My friends, take heart! No, my friends, no more tears! Be unafraid!" someone shouted. It was a man's voice, steady and full of the same cheer that Jonathan once recognized in his own.

Weakly, Jonathan pushed himself from the ground and turned toward the speaker. He was a spectacled man in an army dress uniform. His bearing was proud, too proud to go along with the crutches that grew out of his wiry arms or the way his flaccid legs dragged through the mud.

"Now is the time for rejoicing, for today we are delivered!"

The man swept the crowd with his gaze and smiled so placidly that Jonathan cursed. For the first time in his life, he understood the contempt that the other patients must have held him in whenever he uttered his hopeful inanities. He had never laid eyes on the man before, never come into contact with him in any way, but he hated him with a passion. One smile was all it took.

"Friends, no more will we be afflicted—not you with typhoid, or you with consumption. I will not be done in by polio! Not as an enfeebled cripple will I meet my end! Not as a victim will I perish, but as a hero! We will all be heroes this day, thank God! Heroes to beleaguered Baltimore, to all of America!"

Many in the crowd began to jeer him. Others ignored him, and refocused their attentions on their own hurts and those of their neighbors. Some who could walk began to peel away from the main group, heading in whatever direction they thought best. But as the man continued his oration, Jonathan began to think that he was more than just a deluded fool. A hideous rumor that he had once heard and had tried to forget jumped instantly to the front of his mind. A chill from more than just the autumn air ran down his spine.

"Why flee, my friends? You flee only from glory! Who among you has not prayed, as I have, that some way might be found to defeat the invaders? We have it! My friends, it is you! We are the weapon of our foe's downfall!"

Suddenly, that uncanny droning noise returned, only now it was close at hand. Now that he could hear it more clearly, Jonathan recognized in it a kinship to the sound of the coal-fired tugs, the motorized pumps, and all the din of machinery that filled the harbor. More fluid and less throaty than the engines he knew, but an engine all the same. An ear-piercing whine followed, quickly returned by one of lower pitch. Jonathan's hand tightened on a bare rock as he slowly pushed himself up. Before he could turn in the direction of the sounds, someone else bawled, "Tripods! Tripods!"

"Harvesters!" shouted the cripple. He was insanely jubilant, laughing raucously and calling out to the Martians. Jonathan staggered to his side.

"What do you mean?" Jonathan demanded.

The other man didn't answer. Jonathan grabbed him roughly and shook him free of his crutches. He looked up at Jonathan, who shouted more fiercely. "What did you mean, sir, by calling us weapons? How do we defeat the invaders? Speak up! Tell us what to do!"

The man laughed. "Nothing! We need do nothing at all! The Martians will do it to themselves!"

Less than a dozen yards behind them, the first of the tripods stooped, its metal coils lashing themselves around helpless bodies, constricting them so tightly that men fainted and excrement from their voided bowels rained down. Other captives squirmed desperately, even though to escape the grip of those mighty tentacles so high in the air meant certain death.

"You're a lunatic!"

"Not at all, sir! I understand things perfectly! In fact, I am the one who came up with the idea." The cripple's voice was full of pride and excitement. "I was at the field hospital outside of Wilmington when they attacked. I saw what they did to the captives. I escaped, but the memory—dear God, I can never forget! Only later did I understand why I was permitted to see those horrors and live. It was the key to their defeat! I saw how useless men and horses and cannons were against them, but a doctor knows there are other weapons upon the earth!"

Jonathan began to shake with fury and terror. "You're feeding us to them? Feeding us to them, hoping they get sick!" As if in reply to his own question, Jonathan coughed, and a spray of bloody saliva splashed onto the cripple's cheek. "You... you bastard! You wretched, evil—"

"Please understand! At first we tried emptying the mortuaries. But they won't eat the dead. This was the only way. Tell me, isn't this better than dying in squalor, for nothing? Don't you want to die a hero?"

The cripple hit the mud with a splash. His dented skull landed crookedly, dark blood pooling from the gash above his ear. Jonathan dropped the bloody rock onto the man's chest.

As the tendrils of the harvester coiled around Jonathan's waist, his diseased body destined for the great mesh collecting basket forty feet above, he remembered all that Dr. Barret had told him months ago about the health benefits of "clean, cool air and wholesome victuals." He hoped the opposite held true as well.

Michael is an award-winning author of science fiction and heroic adventure tales. Alongside his wife, Shell, he has written six books set in the Ascension Epoch universe, a world where the emergence of paranormal talents and the invasion of H.G. Wells' Martians in the 19th century have led to a radically transformed present. These works draw heavily from public domain literature and comics and are released under Creative Commons. Find his works at ascensionepoch.com.

Raven9
by George Donnelly

Raven Number 9. My streets, my city, my prey. Mine. I alone defend it now. For the ancestors!

***

"It was all black!" Rona pushed herself against the wall behind a dusty, bannerless stairwell and sobbed.

"Relax." Dane tapped his ear. "Wolf to Roundhouse. Come in." He paused but no answer came back.

The deep guttural throom of the floating vehicle zoomed toward them.

Rona threw herself into Dane. "You said it would be in and out. You said—"

Dane pushed her back into the corner behind the stairwell and grimaced. He charged his weapon. "I'll take care of it."

***

I bear the mission of the ancestors. Will defend, destroy, wipe out. Do you approve, ancestors? Respond.

***

After the noise stopped, Rona peeked an eye out from behind the staircase. Dane's body lay in the debris-strewn street like a flat tire, its legs folded back on themselves, its face a rubber mask of anguish, black tire treads running across the forehead and cheeks. Puddles of goo oozed from razed eye sockets. She recoiled deeper into her hiding place.

You're gonna die here!

Her hands jittered. She stood up, her balance precarious, and walked the few steps to the edge of the darkening street. "You worthless heap of scrap! He was a good man! They all were. You're evil! Bad! Wrong!"

***

Raven9 requires guidance. Destroyed invaders per orders. Told did wrong, was bad. Need instructions, confirmation. Ancestors?

***

Rona looked around the corner. The sleek black beast hung millimeters above the rubbly ground, still and silent. She stuck her arm out and waved. No response. Her heart fluttered.

You're going to get yourself killed!

The short, busty scientist burst out of her hiding spot and ran towards the beta site. She tapped her chest. "Rona to *Arclight*. I need transport!"

Her chest rose and fell. Fetid dust permeated her mouth and desperate breath burned her throat.

A circular pool of air shimmered ahead of her. Her energy flagged, legs heavier, lungs aching. She urged her short limbs on.

The atmosphere rattled around her. Dust flew and the planet spun. All feeling lost, her mind struggled to assign meaning to the black four-legged thing entering the shimmering pool.

***

Lights. Too much. Hurt. No sky, hard cage. Not the ancestors. Hate me. Destroy them. Consume. Kill and destroy.

***

Rona spit dust from her mouth. She moved her knee to stand and a cacophony of pain erupted from all parts. *The portal. My team. My God!*

It sparkled not ten meters from her. She jerked her hand forward into a pile of powdery rubble. A shining disk reflected the light of Beta Persei into her eye and she flinched.

She crawled forward. The thick, heavy disk filled the palm of her hand. The beast, its four legs fully extended, its head upright and proud, occupied the center in relief. Squiggles surrounded it.

The dark giant of the binary system passed in front of its smaller blue brother. Night fell over the street, shadows reaching their misshapen arms to grasp her.

Rona bit into the pain, limped forward and threw herself through the portal.

***

Done, masters. Enemies dead. What's this? Another? Again? Destroy. Con—

***

The beast flew at Rona from across the bridge, its deep throom vibrating, a solid, rectangular block of glowing pitch blackness.

Her teeth clacked. The sound seemed to come from inside her now.

Her palm faced outward at the dog, her fingers grasping the heavy disk.

The beast smoothed now. Curves emerged. A thin rectangle cropped up out of the front of its snaky torso. Four legs extended down and alighted on the bloody metal deck of the ESS *Arclight*.

A wave of nausea blew up inside of Rona and she crashed to the floor.

Master?

The words intruded on her mind. *At rest.* The thought popped into her awareness and she willed it at the beast.

Its legs retracted. The torso descended to the floor. The stick-like head remained attentive.

Rona grinned. She lifted the disk to her face. The beast's head followed.

***

Ancestors returned! New master. Serve you. Yours. Love you, worship you. Do what you say. Only you. Forever. Beautiful. What now? What now? What now?

***

Adventure coming. Rona directed the thought at the prostrate beast.

Its torso rose slightly and its head quivered.

She stepped over Offner, the navigator. Dead, his neck ripped open and crushed. Blood still trickled from the gaping wound. She punched up the navigation charts, her back turned to the creature.

A chill breeze hit her from behind and she froze. *Is this it?* It glided past her and took up station again in front of her, waiting, guarding.

Is it living? Machine? Does it have feelings? Rona set those worries aside. Only one course now. She found the planet, programmed the Navcomp and engaged.

A shower of sparks erupted on the viewscreen, then the cloudless, empty brown surface of MZ458-C.

Rona glanced at the beast. *Master. What now?* Its words and frenetic emotions beat like a drum under her temples.

She opened a portal, the air shimmering behind the beast, a dry heat searing her eyes.

Go through. Check for enemies. Will follow. She willed the words to it. Her stomach throbbed and her hands shook.

The beast rose, its legs hit the floor and its head took a proud angle. *Will protect Master. Love Master. Alone no more.* It turned and jumped through the opening without hesitation.

Rona's relief mixed with the creature's transferred joy. She tapped the nav panel, then collapsed next to it.

***

Raven9 analyzed the blue star. It was hotter than the previous one. He adjusted his operating parameters to maintain a safe internal temperature.

Master? He sat and awaited her arrival. He had a good feeling about this one. He'd already proven his worth. She was different.

The shimmering circle closed, disappeared. Far above him, sparks exploded.

Master?

George Donnelly is the author of space opera, robot apocalypse and dystopian science fiction series. A rebel and unreformed idealist, he believes equally in human rights and abundant hugs before bedtime. Get a new free short story every month at georgedonnelly.com.

Welcome to the Neighborhood
by Allan Davis

"Wow. I had no idea the homeowner association fees would be so high."

The attorney paused in his paper-shuffling. "It helps if you don't think of them as fees," he said, with an air of practice that made it obvious he was repeating the phrase for the thousandth time. "Ah, well, I'm sorry, I forgot you were from out of state. Did the realtor even show you around the community?"

"No, I haven't seen much of it at all, except for the drive in from the gate."

"Well, then, let's take a break from the signatures, and I will be happy to show you around myself." He stacked the papers neatly, stood, and gestured towards the door.

Outside, the morning sun was shining as he led his client down the street. After a few short blocks, they came to a sparkling lake.

"It's huge, and beautiful."

"And it makes for a great border," the lawyer said. "There's one just like it out on the west side of the neighborhood, too." He turned, and they strode side by side away from the water, past a wide variety of homes all fronted by perfectly immaculate lawns.

"This does seem like a great place to live," the client said.

"Oh, it is. I've been here all my life. And your HOA fees cover the cost of so many things here. For example, if someone falls on hard times, they can apply for free food."

"Oh, that's nice," said the client. "A safety net, to help people get back on their feet?"

"Exactly." They strode past the local elementary school. "We also have our own schools, so the fees go to pay the teachers and administrators. Not to mention the textbooks and course curricula; the HOA has experts that put all of that together for us. They make sure that all of the kids get exactly the same quality education."

As they passed the high school, the lawyer continued. "We also have to pay for the buses and the weapons."

"I'm sorry," the client interrupted, "but did you say weapons?"

"Yes, I did. Every now and then they gather up all of the fifteen and sixteen year olds, hand them baseball bats and chains, and bus them off to beat the snot out of the people in another neighborhood."

The client was aghast. "Why the heck would you want to do something like that?"

"Isn't it obvious? To keep them from busing their people out here, of course." At the look of confusion and concern on the man's face, he added "and don't worry, all of the kids come back, safe and sound. Well, almost all of them. Mostly. Anyway."

They walked in silence for a long while after that. The attorney seemed content to let the client observe and learn without any added comments.

The client pointed out a dish high over the houses. "I assume you get internet via satellite here?"

"Huh? Oh, no, that's not internet. That's a listening post."

"Listening? You mean they spy on you?"

"Oh, I wouldn't really call it spying," the lawyer answered. "They monitor phone calls and email. It's a tool to help them spot those busloads before they get here. Though," he added, a bit quieter, "I think they also use them for other stuff. Like preventing robberies, catching crooks, chasing down people who cheat on their HOA fees, stuff like that."

"How could you possibly cheat on your HOA fees? I mean…you either pay them or you don't, right…?"

"Oh, no, your fees are on a sliding scale," the lawyer said. "The more you make, the higher your fees. After all, the more money you bring in, the more likely you are to use all of the benefits of the neighborhood, so it just makes sense that you should pay more. There's even a point on the low end of the scale where people who make too little actually get paid instead of having to pay, so there's an incentive to cheat built right in."

They waited for a few slow-moving cars to pass and crossed the street, and walked around a large building with flags flying. Behind the building, there was a row of twelve cages, eleven of them occupied. The people inside looked sullen and bored.

"Here, I can show you that we take your safety seriously. We lock away all of the dangerous people to make sure the neighborhood is safe." After a moment's pause, he added "I'm going to have to send in a second request for another row of cells; we're just about full."

"That's quite a level of security. What did they do to get locked up?"

"Oh, the usual. Burglary, rape, attempted murder. Those two there tried to cheat on their HOA fees, and the three on the end grew the wrong plants."

The client stopped dead in his tracks. "Wait. Did you say...plants?"

"Yes. The HOA is very specific about the kinds of plants you can grow. Heck, those three will be in those cages longer than the two who cheated on their HOA fees."

The lawyer led the way back towards his office. "Like I was saying, it helps if you don't think of them as fees, or taxes, or anything negative like that. If you think of them more as dues, it helps. They cover the costs of all of the cool things the HOA does for the people who live here."

When they reached the steps leading up to the door of the attorney's office, the client said, "You know, I think I'm about ready to finish up those papers now."

"Good! I'm glad to hear it." He held the door open for his client to step through first. "You're going to love living here."

By the time the attorney reached his desk, the client was indeed finished with the papers—the last shreds of them were falling through the air, scattering around the office like snowflakes.

By day, Allan is a mild-mannered computer geek. But by night...he creates worlds so the other people who live in his mind have somewhere to play. Science fiction, fantasy, and horror spew out of the dark and twisted corners of his brain, with political rants or humorous work thrown in just to keep people guessing. Never, under any circumstances, allow him to sing after midnight. Or before midnight. Find his works at allandavisjr.blogspot.com.

Chip Doc
by William F. Wu

In the bright lights of the spare operating room, Dr. Eng worked on the patient with one scrub nurse and a number of outdated electronic machines blinking and beeping. Through a sealed window, two freed rebels watched him as always. As he had done countless times before, he focused on the brain of the patient, carefully searching for the neurochip that received mind-control orders from government transmitters and then automatically sent out information in response. As he worked, his own mind functioned just as automatically while he listened to an old folksong:

"The hour was sad, I left the maid,
A lingering farewell taking;
Her sighs and tears my steps delayed,
I thought my heart was breaking.
In hurried words her name I blest,
I breathed the vows that bind me
And to my heart in anguish pressed
The girl I left behind me."

In Dr. Eng's hands, the instruments sought out the chip inside the patient's brain. While part of his forebrain sang, another part of his brain understood the work his hands had to do.

***

Jarod 319 stood next to Patya 1222, watching the operating room through the sealed window. They were a generation younger than Dr. Eng and took part in the risky, violent maneuvers of the rebellion. "We'll have one more freed rebel to join the fight," said Jarod 319.

"He can free anyone." Patya 1222 spoke in awe. "No one else can. At least, no one else in the rebellion."

"No one else." Jarod 319's fingertips touched the scar on his head, under his short, brown hair, left after Dr. Eng had removed Jarod 319's neurochip. All the freed rebels dropped their surnames after their chips were removed.

***

"Chickens crowin' on Sourwood Mountain,
    Hey de-ing dang diddle alley day.
    So many pretty girls I can't count 'em,
    Hey de-ing dang diddle alley day."
Dr. Eng leaned forward from the waist and the flexible nutrition tube that fed him through an arm vein shifted with him. His hands located the patient's neurochip.

***

Patya 1222 drew in a breath. "He has the neurochip. Everything looks good." She, too, felt the scar on her scalp, underneath her blunt-cut, shiny black hair.

"He's always good," said Jarod 319. He watched the scrub nurse, who was attentive but unworried. "It makes me sad."

"Me, too," said Patya, blinking back tears.

***

The plucked strings of a koto ran through Dr. Eng's mind, at a calming pace, as he disconnected the neurochip. He focused on the melody while his hands took the neurochip out of the patient's brain and set it on a tray.

***

Jarod 319 nodded approval. "That's one more chip we can use."

"What kind of misdirection are we planning next?" Patya 1222 asked.

"We'll transmit disinformation about our upcoming attack on the Galveston arsenal," said Jarod 319.

"Excellent. I'll lead a squad in that assault."

***

The finish to 1812 Overture, Op. 49, by Pyotr Ilyich Tchaikovsky, sent cannons booming and snare drums firing muskets through Dr. Eng's mind as he closed his patient's scalp. After the overture ended, the chip in Dr. Eng's brain, programmed to shuffle files, began a Tibetan Buddhist chant in male voices at a very low pitch.

***

Patya 1222 watched as two attendants wheeled the patient out a rear door to a recovery room, followed by the scrub nurse. Then she pushed in front of Jarod and led the way through the main doors. She took Dr. Eng's makeshift wooden wheelchair from a corner and hurried it forward. Dr. Eng was still standing, now motionless.

When Patya 1222 had the wheelchair positioned, Jarod 319 disconnected the nutrition tube and gently drew the surgeon down into the chair.

She wheeled Dr. Eng out of the operating room and up the hall with Jarod. Curious, she touched a button on the top edge of the wheelchair's back.

A receiver built into the chair picked up the signal from the neurochip in Dr. Eng's brain and quietly played the Tibetan chant.

The rebellion's intelligence wing had reported that enemy agents were convinced he had gone over the edge because when they played his chip transmission, they never found anything resembling human thought.

"I hope he's not fed up with the files," said Jarod 319.

Patya 1222 sighed. "We'll never know."

All the rebels knew Dr. Eng had chosen the files himself, to occupy his forebrain for as long as he lived. Patya and several others could theoretically program more files into Dr. Eng's neurochip, but he had been adamant about personally choosing the sounds and sights that would fill his mind for the rest of his tightly circumscribed life.

"I hope the government spies got fed up long ago." Jarod 319 gave a short, bitter chuckle.

Patya 1222 remained silent as she walked.

Dr. Eng wanted to free as many rebels as possible of their embedded neurochips, so he had to maintain his ability to remove them surgically. He could not remove his own, of course, and neither could any other rebel. Yet none of them could prevent his neurochip from transmitting information to the government surveillance analysts. So, to disguise his actions and location, he had used nanotech in his blood to program his own chip. It now allowed him only to perform a certain set of surgeries, but do little else. He could no longer converse, feed himself, shower, or use the restroom on his own, so he needed dedicated caretakers.

His programming flooded his mind with harmless entertainment: Music, recorded lectures, performances of comedies and dramas, even soothing sounds from nature. These recordings were the only transmissions that his neurochip sent out.

It worked, at the cost of Dr. Eng living a full life.

Patya 1222 leaned down close and whispered, though she doubted he could hear her: "I love you, Daddy."

William F. Wu is one of the writers in the Wild Cards *anthology series, edited by George R.R. Martin, and has an ongoing series of stories in the* War World *anthologies edited by John F. Carr of Pequod Press. Wu is a 6-time nominee for the Hugo, Nebula, and World Fantasy Awards. His backlog of work is going online gradually as ebooks, available from most ebook retailers. Find his works at williamfwu.com.*

Garbin's Honor
by George Donnelly

"I wish to board the shuttle to Gottverden. I have a grievance to present to the Kamra and I have every proxy on Verroche."

"Every proxy? That's impossible. Not even Ziin, much less any other god, could collect every proxy." The ship's steward blocked his path.

Garbin's ten thousand zone leaders stood at a safe distance behind him. He swallowed and they seemed to take a collective step back. Their shoulders hunched and their faces fell.

Garbin straightened his back, cleared his throat and met the ship's steward's buzzard eyes. "Indeed, it was thought impossible. But thanks to my ten thousand zone leaders and thanks to the righteousness of my cause — indeed, even you would sign your proxy on if—"

"I do not have a vote."

Garbin took a deep breath and steeled himself once more. "Indeed, but if you did, even you would see the righteousness of my cause, a fundamental flaw in our universal system of law that calls into question every—"

"Just show me the proxies."

The steward seemed shorter now. He did not meet Garbin's eyes anymore. He reached into the pockets of his long, gray coat. He sniffed, as if about to cry and at once Garbin noted the peculiar inconsistencies of the man. The gray coat was impeccable at the front, but frayed and stained at the sides. His face was neatly shaved and his hair finely combed above his forehead. But on the sides it became unruly — runaway curls bordered by an unshaven neck.

A man such as this serving the legateurs? Garbin handed him his comtrer and crossed his arms.

His zone leaders seemed to be gone. Not a sound of theirs reached him. The entire platform must be deserted. Beyond it, behind Garbin's back, rose the great peak of Verroche, Mont Origl. At its apex, his home hunkered, an abandoned mass of logs and overgrown gardens. He'd left his self-imposed isolation ten years ago and not been back.

He was guaranteed return now.

The steward scrolled through Garbin's records. His record-keeping device beeped, again and again. The steward shook his head and handed the comtrer back to Garbin. "You have some questionable proxies in there, but—"

"I can assure you, sir. Every proxy was received with the complete and informed consent of—"

"Quiet." The steward looked at his wrist. "I could reject you simply for being late."

"I arrived three days early."

"But your contemporaries arrived four days early. They

are already on the shuttle and guaranteed a hearing of their grievance in the Kamra of Ziin. You, however…"

Gottverden rolled across the sky from behind the steward's right ear. Orange and purple in the twilight sky, Gottverden sat massive above his home planet. He was lucky to have Gottverden so close. He knew that. Some in the distant galaxies had to travel lifetimes to present their grievances. Many dropped dead upon arrival in the Kamra, ecstatic to have reached the culmination of centuries of organizing and planning.

Garbin opened his mouth to beg, then reconsidered. He *was* Verroche. Ten billion people did not beg. They demanded. "All of my papers are in order and the people of Verroche demand—"

"The trip to Gottverden is a one-way trip. Do you understand that?"

"Unless—"

"You will either meet with success and return to a normal life or be marooned permanently on Gottverden, an object of shame and contempt, to live in want and exile, for the rest of your life, never able to leave, never able to see your loved ones again. This is Ziin's Bargain. Do you understand that?"

"I have no loved ones."

"Your life may be optioned for service to the Kamra at any time after you inevitably fail. Only one claim in the last five thousand years has met with success. Do you understand that?"

Garbin wanted to return home, to his shack on Mont

Origl. A simple life, a life of honor, close to the land. He dreamt of it. He needed it. His supporters had fled. He could plead to them that the steward was unfair, a hard man. He opened his mouth.

But the fatal flaw. The legateurs must know of it. His people must be freed from it. He had discovered it. He had taught his people of it. He bore the responsibility for it. He'd chosen a path. To diverge from it now would be weakness and dishonor. It was the attempt that mattered. The honor came from it, an unblemishable honor, no matter what might follow. No matter his degree of success or failure, no matter what they might say of him later.

"I understand."

A sly smile crept across the steward's face. He stepped aside. The shuttle door slid open.

Two rows of two seats each ran from behind the shuttle driver's seat to the back, not holding more than twenty passengers. Every one was full and a handful stood. Garbin recognized none of them. He had spoken to so many Verroche over the last decade. He had their proxies, all of them. Of that he was sure. Some of them likely had his as well. But not one of them met his eyes.

He found a spot next to a tall, dark-skinned man and grabbed hold of a supple strap.

"I'm Garbin Frigard." He offered his hand.

The man turned away and walked to the back of the shuttle.

He approached the next man, a short, stocky fellow with a hungry yet confused look. "Hi, I'm—"

"We all know who you are. You hold all of our proxies and are the best candidate for achieving rectification in five thousand years." The stocky man wiped his nose and turned away.

"Quiet!" The steward stepped in and the door slid shut behind him. He opened a tiny panel in the wall and pressed a button.

The shuttle jumped away from the edge of the platform and hung there. The floor turned transparent.

The great expanse of stars fell away below his feet, like a swath of irregular paint applied to a pockmarked surface by a defective brush. One big white ball stuck out from the rest. Too bright, he looked away from it.

A new pair of feet, these ones bare, entered his view.

A bearded young man, his hair shaven to the scalp, his eyes blue, elbowed him and looked behind Garbin. "See that mountain? They say there is a legend. Someday, someone from such a humble place will bring a great change to the universe, one that not even the wise and wonderful Ziin can foresee."

"Don't believe every legend you hear!" the steward yelled.

Garbin smiled at the young man. "I know." He surveyed his fellow grevers. "We're going to Gottverden, friends! The legateurs will hear our claims! Rejoice!"

"Quiet down!" the steward growled. "Or I'll end you faster than you can summon your proxies."

***

"You can't do that here. It's forbidden by law."

"Don't worry, sir, I am almost done."

The navy-blue-suited gendarme pulled a black stick from his belt and slapped it against the palm of his opposing hand. "The Kamra is very clear on this matter. There is no campaigning on Gottverden. You will stop now or—"

Garbin secured the last grever's thumbprint on his comtrer, bowed and turned to the gendarme, the great golden dome of the Kamra beckoning from behind him.

Another gendarme, this one wearing green, tapped the first one on the shoulder and wagged his finger at him. The first gendarme retreated.

"I do apologize, Grever Frigard. I didn't..."

Garbin opened his mouth to congratulate the man. He was upholding the law after all. A screeching, crunching howl sounded behind him and he turned.

The shuttles lined up one after another, spewing out their grevers in tight clumps. A shuttle emptied and moved forward. The first in line entered a roofed area, just tall enough for it. The roof fell and the floor rose. The howl repeated and the craft disappeared, replaced by a thin sheet of metal that clattered down beneath the platform out of sight.

Garbin shuddered. They really meant it. There was no going back. He turned to the gendarme. "Do they destroy all ships like that?"

The man raised an arm as if to shield himself from an oncoming blow. His face tightened. He nodded and trotted away.

The bearded youth bounded up to Garbin. "I'm Ragfrar, by the way." He extended his hand with a wide, white grin. "What's your grievance?"

Garbin took the boy's hand and squeezed it. But the boy's grip was weak and he felt disgust. The great press crushed another shuttle and Garbin shuddered.

"Mine's about the—"

Garbin waved him to silence. Between him and the press, a great sculpture rose from the ground. A pointed square rose from a semi-circle base, with a dozen wavy arms reaching in all directions to represent the reach of the Gottverden Kamra. Near its base, a face looked out. Strong but clean, it was Ziin, father to the gods and benefactor of Gottverden. Or so the legend told.

"It's a weapon, you know, the Olindama." The boy stepped closer to him. His breath stank of rotten parseils and rancid trufnix.

Did people give him their proxy out of pity? "What is your grievance?"

"The standard of sanitation, my dad says, is just not up to—"

Garbin walked to the sculpture. He caressed it with his palm. Completely smooth. He rapped it with his knuckle. Hard, like rock. He circled it. Directly opposite from the press, a circular hole crawled deep into the structure. Next to it was a thin keyhole.

Garbin inserted his hand. He gripped a handle and pulled on it. But there was no give.

"Only the gods themselves can do anything with it. Not

even the legateurs. They say it's a weapon, crafted by Ziin himself." The boy leaned in, his mouth open, sweat sparkling on his brow.

"How did you get here anyway?" The press crushed another shuttle behind Garbin and he stopped himself from looking.

A three-armed grever stepped off a shuttle and veered towards Garbin. Five eyes blinked at once and the mouth spread into a leer. It held up a finger, then manipulated its comtrer. A tinny voice popped from nearby.

"I have an important issue of interest to the people of your planet and humbly request a chance to win your proxies. Will you hear me?"

Garbin shook his head then caught himself. Just minutes ago, he was doing the same thing. He would listen to this... beast. "Go ahead."

Gendarmes sprinted from the receiving station across the way. "Stop! Stop that! You may not campaign—"

Garbin extended a hand to stop them.

One gendarme skidded to a halt in front of him. Three more passed and one grabbed each of the beast's arms.

"I'm willing to hear him out. Please don't—"

"So sorry, Grever Frigard. Our sincerest apologies. We'll take care of this." The gendarme strode over to the beast, arms straight at the elbows. He drew his black stick, beat the thing over the head and kicked it to the ground.

"I am a credentialed grever from the Aryxxgik galaxy. You cannot..." The tinny voice petered out. The gendarmes dragged him to the receiving station.

The boy grabbed Garbin's arm above the elbow and pulled him toward the receiving station. "Same way you did, Garbin. I got some proxies and found an important issue. You're probably wondering why they picked me. I mean, look at me, I'm a mess. Well, I volunteered. Nobody else wanted to go. All I have is my dad after all, no girl, no kids, mom died. I've never been no good to anyone and this is my chance to do something and, well, here I am, eh, Garbin? You and me, very cool, huh?"

Garbin stopped and turned around. The sculpture. He had to touch it again. The last grevers poured from the last shuttle and he had to have their proxies. He looked back at the gendarmes. No sign of them. He strode forward.

His ear tingled. His comtrer shook. A woman's face appeared on it, the leader of his planet.

"We're so proud of you, Garbin Frigard. The people of Verroche owe you a debt of gratitude that can never be repaid." The woman's fake smile rankled his soul. It might even be a recording, played for the grevers of Verroche over and over again. They didn't believe in him. Only one in five thousand years had made it.

The statistics would change because of him. He would be number two. Because the alternative was unthinkable.

***

Garbin rubbed his hands together. His stomach jumped and twisted. He passed through the inner doorway of the Kamra. He'd present his claim. He'd win. The entire galaxy would know of his success and of the great victory of Verroche.

"If you win, they'll give you a certificate. That's how you'll know. Got it?" His ship's steward pursed his lips. "Did everyone get that?"

"What happens if we lose?" Ragfrar rubbed his nose and drew in breath. His eyes darted from side to side.

"You're on the street, on your own. Find a gang and you'll be fine. There's always new openings. I'm gonna be straight with you guys. That's your fate. You came here to stay."

"Can we get a job like yours?" Ragfrar asked.

The steward shook his head. "Ineligible. Now. You'll go up to that podium over there. You'll read your grievance and state your proxy percentage. Red light means no. Green light means yes. Got it? Get in line. Ziin watches you. Do not embarrass yourselves."

The other grevers pushed and shoved. Garbin found himself at the end of the line, right behind Ragfrar. The Kamra was huge. Perfectly circular, the legateurs sat high up above them in banks and rows he couldn't see. The circle was cut into four equal slices and four sunken entry corridors ran into the heart of the Kamra, a small disc from which the Dewan presided and the grevers made known their grievances.

One by one, the grevers from each of the four lines inched towards the podium. They merged at the center and climbed the spiral staircases that encircled the podium.

A red light reflected off the arching roof of the Kamra

and cast a deathly glow into the eyes of his contemporaries. The legateurs turned another supplicant away. Then another.

Ragfrar climbed the last step of the spiraling staircase and stepped to the podium. A long light bulb hung from a rope above the boy's head, as if it were a guillotine about to fall. He looked back at the Dewan.

Grass-green and citrox-yellow robes flowed from the man's neck to his feet. An intricate, triangle, square and semi-circle pattern repeated vertically, with hands reaching out in all directions. A thin, arched hat of similar material sat on the top of his head.

Garbin shuddered. The dress was ugly. It was the first time he'd seen a legateur and he wasn't impressed. The robes obscured his still body but the face, although hairless, was like any other human's.

The Dewan motioned to Ragfrar. Ragfrar faced ahead and cleared his throat.

"I am here—" He dug deep into his lungs and coughed once more. His knees locked and opened. "I am here about the sanitation on my home world of Verroche." He spat the words and spittle flew with them, illuminated by the overhead lights.

"Your proxy percentage." The Dewan barely moved but Garbin caught the outlines of arms and legs under the robe.

"Zero point zero zero—"

A flutter arose from the Kamra. Garbin stepped up to get a better look but the steward pulled him back down. The light flashed red. Ragfrar's eyes shot to Garbin, his face loose. The floor underneath him withdrew and the boy disappeared.

"Get going already." The steward pushed him.

Garbin stepped onto the platform. The old wood creaked under his foot. A smooth groove was worn into the step. How many had placed their feet here before him? How many times had the Kamra steps been rebuilt? Five-thousand years is a long time. He scanned for blank certificates or even a machine to spit them out but there was nothing. His stomach tightened.

The Dewan inclined his head towards the podium. Garbin cleared his throat and stepped up to it.

"For five-thousand years there has been a fatal flaw at the root of Gottverden law. It has been there since the very beginning, from the very first, founding document of our universal system of law. I, Garbin Frigard, come to you today, to rectify this flaw, so that we might have five-thousand more years of balance, peace and prosperity—"

"Proxy percentage!"

The chamber was dark. He heard flutters and creaks out there but saw no face, no body. He looked behind him and to his sides. Everywhere it was the same. Darkness where he expected legateurs. Illuminated legateurs. Intelligent legateurs who would hear his words and congratulate him for his ingenuity, his persistence, his intelligence and courage.

"One hundred point zero zero percent," Garbin said.

A click sounded above and a great light shone on a seat in the first row of the Kamra.

"That's impossible!"

Garbin looked across at the legateur. Silky locks of golden hair fell to his temples. Perfectly smooth skin framed slate blue eyes. His chest tightened.

"It's true, I—"

"Why, not one of us has garnered more than one percent—" A whistling noise came from farther back and the legateur quieted.

The Dewan was at his side, revising his comtrer. He scrolled up and down. He refreshed the proxy count. He looked up at the legateur and nodded.

"How did you do it?" The legateur ran his hands down his thin white robe.

Garbin looked at the Dewan. The Dewan inclined his head and stepped away. "I have worked on this matter my entire life. As a boy, my father gave me law books. I read them all. I found the fatal flaw after ten years of study. Ten years later, I stand before you having collected every proxy in the universe."

"You campaigned illegally at the dock, did you not?"

Garbin blinked.

The legateur smiled and raised his arms in a gesture of greeting. "You cheated. But you cheated well, and very effectively." He turned his back to Garbin. "Who among us has not cheated a little in order to get here?" He turned back around and clapped.

Garbin swallowed. *Congratulating me for cheating? Why is it illegal anyway?*

The entire Kamra joined the legateur in clapping, a

thunderous cacophony of concussions that came from everywhere and inside of him all at once.

A great heat welled up in him. He wanted to cry and laugh at the same time. He looked back at the Dewan. He was not preparing a certificate. He looked up at the light. It flashed neither red nor green. He looked back at the now fully illuminated Kamra. They stood for him and cheered. It was only a matter of time.

"Tell us more of this flaw." The legateur in the front row glanced at his wrist.

"Do I receive a certificate now? And the green light?"

The Dewan appeared next to him, his brows lowered, shaking his head. "Patience, my son."

The legateur in the front row motioned for Garbin to continue.

"The flaw has existed since the very beginning. The law is based on the consent of the governed. But there is no mechanism for—"

A great clang sounded. More lights burst into full illumination. Garbin covered his eyes. A great fluttering sounded around him.

He pried one eye open. Neither green nor red, the light above him was. The Dewan was gone. The Kamra was empty. The lights clicked off and darkness surrounded him.

***

"Why did you abandon me in there?"

"My dear boy, it was three o'clock, the end of the

business day here on Gottverden. That is simply one of our many customs. I thought you had prepared diligently to come here."

Garbin scanned the meeting hall. Long tables ran in two columns from the front to the distant back. It'd been a long, slow slog to get out of the Kamra in the dark. This place sat right next to the side exit. And there was the legateur from the Kamra, sitting at the bar.

"I was told I would get a certificate and the green light would be illuminated. And, may I ask your name please?"

The blond-locked legateur flashed him a wide smile. "Me? I'm Snorre, permanent representative of the great world of Xerixon, in the Andromeda Galaxy. How about a drink? It's in your honor, after all, that all of the legateurs of the Kamra assemble here tonight."

A small glass appeared in front of Garbin, an amber liquid occupying the full volume. He sniffed it and took a sip. "Water?"

Snorre laughed. A glass of water appeared at Garbin's hand and he drank.

"Legateur Snorre—"

"Just Snorre. You are among peers now, Garbin." Snorre rested a hand on his shoulder and squeezed.

"I was told a certificate was granted and the green light would—"

Snorre shook his head at him with a look half-irritated, half-scoffing. "This is for ordinary men. Not for men who hold the power of the universe in their comtrers." He downed another drink in one shot. "We haven't lit the green light in fifty centuries. Maybe longer. Does it even work anymore? Ziin knows!" He laughed and took another shot. "Please, dear Garbin, drink more." He passed him another glass.

Garbin took another, tiny sip of his first drink. A mighty legateur speaking with him, like this, he daren't disrespect the man. But drink was not for him. "The certificate. I need to show my people, the Verroche."

"Damnit, man!" Snorre slammed his fist into the bar and the room quieted. "Don't you understand? You hold the power of the universe in your comtrer. You could abolish the Kamra, put us all out of jobs here, do anything you liked! Why—"

"Shut up, Snorre!" a dozen voices yelled simultaneously.

"But I don't wish to do that. I only wish to see the flaw rectified. And to return to Verroche, to my shack on Mont Origl. I only need the cert—"

Snorre slammed his hand over the grever's mouth. He whispered. "Six hundred years I have craved power like yours. Six hundred years I have been denied. My proxies expire and I may not leave this world, nor advance in the Kamra. And you sit here talking of a pathetic piece of paper! Damn you. Damn you. You are a fool and do not deserve this power. Damn you!" He snapped his fingers.

Power like mine? Six hundred years?

The doors behind Garbin flew open. Glass broke. Legateurs scattered. Men in dirty clothes, their hair uncut, their faces unshaven and their eyes wild with hunger poured through. Their eyes fell on Garbin.

Snorre gestured to them, then turned and downed another drink.

The mob flew at him. Heavy hands grabbed his limbs and pulled him out to the street.

***

"I have a note for the Dewan."

"Who would entrust a note for the Dewan to a stinking wreck such as yourself."

"One who sought discretion." Garbin looked up at his old ship's steward. After three months surviving on rotten crumbs and flame-licked furat in the sewage-infected corners of Gottverden, the man no longer seemed quite so mean. He was clean, almost godly himself.

"Go ahead." The steward turned away then looked back. He grabbed Garbin's arm. "Wait, I know you." He narrowed his eyes and scanned his former passenger up and down. "They don't want you in there."

"I must enter. Tonight, my proxies expire."

"Do something for me."

Garbin stood a little taller. He searched his eyes for intention.

"I want to be a member of the Kamra, your new Kamra."

My new Kamra? The words meant nothing to Garbin. He sought only to rectify a flaw in the law. "I will tell them of your righteousness and they will recognize it."

The steward recoiled, a look of disgust on his face. He waved Garbin in.

Garbin stepped into the chilly corridor. Ahead of him, a grever presented his claim. The light turned red and another reached the podium. He strode forward. This time he wouldn't wait in line.

A hand reached out and stopped him. "Is that really you, Garbin of Verroche?"

Garbin's eyes struggled in the gloom.

"It's me Ragfrar, your old friend and compatriot!" He turned Garbin towards the door and put his arm around his shoulders.

Garbin stopped. A purple cape flowed at the boy's back. His beard was gone. His brown locks were impeccable. His eyes remained hungry.

"Oh yes, I've done quite well. My grievance was denied, of course. But a legateur liked my presentation. He gave me a small apartment and I brought a young lady from home. We're very happy now."

"Do you have any food? I... I haven't been—"

"Drop this." The boy bared his teeth and his breathing grew heavy.

Garbin looked at his hands then back at the boy.

"Drop this business. Abandon it. Give up! Don't you see all the resistance you're meeting? It means you must stop. Reevaluate your goals and your course. It's too hard, can't you see it?"

Behind him, the line advanced. The red light flickered again and again.

"Think of your parents, man. Do you wish to cause them disgrace?"

"My parents are dead."

"Then your cousins, aunts and uncles, siblings, old friends, girlfriends, surely you must have a love interest?"

"I sacrificed everything to come here. To rectify the law. As we all did."

"Rectify the law? Listen to yourself. Not even Ziin himself speaks like that. You're ruining—" The boy pulled a bag from his back. It hung by a strap from his shoulders. He rummaged around in it and pulled out a naked baby girl.

A pink ribbon adorned the girl's sparse black hair. Her gray eyes regarded him placidly. She smiled and her four limbs kicked and grabbed as one.

"What about her? Do you like her?" Ragfrar held the girl out to Garbin and he received her. "Because the legateurs will kill her if you persist!"

"Why?" He rocked the girl in his arms. Her body jerked and she shivered. He squatted down, pulled the ragged shirt from his back and wrapped her in it.

The last of the new grevers climbed the central disc now. Garbin pushed past them. He climbed the spiral staircase, the balls of his feet landing half on the black marble steps and half hanging into the dark abyss below. The baby cooed up at him and reached for the growing beard that hung from his chin.

He bounded to the podium.

"I am Garbin Frigard and I hold one hundred percent of the proxies of the universe. I demand my certificate. I demand the green light."

He studied the darkness around him. Yawns, fluttering

and other noises echoed through the great hall. But no spotlight shone. He looked behind him at the Dewan. The man stared straight ahead.

"I demand… I will not allow any further hearing of grievances until mine is attended to."

The next grever in line motioned to him. "Hey, brother, move along. You had your chance and failed, just like everyone else. Give up already. Only five minutes to three. A lot of guys left to be heard. And we can't get appointments if we haven't been denied."

Garbin turned back to the podium. "As holder of one hundred percent of the proxies in the universe, I hereby dissolve this—"

A strong hand grabbed his arm. An oversized comtrer-like device landed in his hands.

"This is for you."

This comtrer rested precipitously on his two outstretched hands. The baby shifted and he adjusted himself to catch the device. Six screens streamed to him his own visage, there in the Kamra, with the baby girl, the same humble grever standing behind him. Six screens, each with its own dial, stared back at him.

"They always win." The steward firmed his grip on Garbin's shoulder. "Even when they lose, by Ziin, they win. Just give up."

On each screen, with slight variations of color and timing, he and the baby girl collapsed to the ground, their eyes bulging and lifeless.

***

"Does it show my life, too?"

"Only the parts with me." Garbin smiled down at Taka. "Go read a book, young one."

"Does it tell us our future?" She pulled herself closer to the table and brushed her long black hair from her face. Her eyes considered him with intelligence and intensity.

Garbin laughed. "Our past is our future, it seems. It shows… our lives, repeating over and over again, countless times, across these universes but always the same events. Too many times to count. And every time, failure." He set the device on the rough-hewn table and turned away. Tears poured from his eyes and that space behind his nose ached.

"But what about this future?" She reached a fat little hand out and rubbed his hairy forearm.

"It stops at the present moment."

"Then we can change it. We can do something different."

"But I've watched it all. I've disassembled and rebuilt the device. I don't know what else to do but the next thing that it shows in our previous life."

"To see the steward?"

Garbin nodded. "Do you have any other ideas?"

"I like it here, with you."

"I want more for you than another ten years of starvation, stuck in a rotting basement, sickness and despair."

"We can leave. Go to Verroche."

53

"There are no ships. I've shown you the grevers' shuttles."

Her face darkened. "What about Legateur Snorre?"

Garbin raised an eyebrow. "Would you trust him again?"

She shook her head.

She was thin, weak. Where had she come from? What happened to Ragfrar? Why did he never see Snorre anymore? He'd snuck into the Kamra a thousand times. The faces changed. But always the same dreary procession of denied grevers. Red light after red light.

Something had to change.

"Grab your peluche. We will see the steward and we may not return." His chair screeched against the cold stone floor. He reached for her hand.

"I don't want to go." Her eyes went thin and water flowed from them. "What about our things, our books?"

"This is trash, all of this. We will do better on Verroche. I will show you my home. It has more books and better ones. I will work and get you many toys, all the—"

"I don't want to go! This is our home!"

He ground his teeth together. He grabbed her peluche, a green creature with six limbs and a too-friendly face. He pulled her from the chair and tucked the device under his arm.

The girl grabbed onto the table. He pried her fingers up and pulled her out the door. She grabbed onto the door frame. He set her down, her soiled toes wriggling against the rough rock.

"There is no future for us here." He looked out into the

street. Floating cameras twirled towards him, their lenses dialing in on his face. People stopped and stared. Men chattered to other men behind guarding hands.

"Would you like a nicer apartment?" A man tugged at Garbin's sleeve and he startled.

"Get away from me." Garbin kneeled down in front of Taka and whispered. "Don't you see. It's dangerous for us. They watch our every move. Others have disappeared."

"But who are *they*?"

Garbin shook his head and sighed. If only he knew. If only he understood how this power of Gottverden worked. He'd spent his life watching this world, first from afar, then through books, after that through the hearts of men desperate for change but afraid to pursue it themselves.

It didn't work the way the books said. Something was wrong. He couldn't change it after all. The flaw, perhaps it was even intentional. He'd tried to remedy it, over and over again, across universes and eons and they always won. But who are *they*?

He grabbed the girl and they flew down the narrow, gray-bricked street. The Kamra was ahead and there was the steward, in his navy-blue, body-length jacket. The faces of the Kamra might change but the gatekeeper remained constant.

"Steward." Corbin let go of Taka and ran to him.

The steward wagged his finger. "You are not permitted entrance here, beggar."

"Steward, you gave me this device ten years ago today. Do you recognize it?"

The steward glanced at the unusually large comtrer, burped and shook his head. "Now move along. You're overdue."

"I need to know what it means. I need to understand."

The steward grabbed the device and whispered. "If you will not put it to use, Garbin Frigard, then let me find another who might do so." He ripped the device away.

Garbin grabbed onto it again. "What do you mean? I need more—"

Gendarmes appeared at the end of the street. They pointed at Garbin and ran, their long arms reaching towards him, pointing again and again.

Garbin grabbed onto the device. "Just a clue. Something. I have studied it for ten years, living from the scraps of this city. Something."

The steward released his grip, a gentle appreciation forming on his face. "Ten years? Good. Do it another ten years. You will see, with Ziin's blessing."

The gendarmes were within arm's reach now. They stopped and readied their weapons.

"Now run!" The steward pointed toward the dock.

***

"Breakfast, Papa."

"Yes, yes."

Garbin sat outside his shack on the slopes of Mont Origl and looked up through a hole in the decaying thatch roof. There, high above the sharp slopes was his home. Now occupied by a man with a wife and four happy children. They ran and danced all day long, screaming, singing and cheering. It was his life they had. If only he'd given up his struggle to rectify the law.

Bitterness grew in his heart and he snuffed it out as a matter of habit. He chose a different destiny. Higher or lower, better or worse, he knew not. Only that this was his path now and stay on it he must.

"Pa, your breakfast." Taka opened the flimsy door and stood in front of him. She handed him the scratched metal plate and set the steaming mug on the windowsill next to him.

"I am not hungry." He set the plate down at his feet. Tiny yellow birds flitted down and hopped towards it.

Taka retrieved the food with an angry flourish. "We have so little!" She retreated back into the shack.

He looked down, past the edge of his land. The next home was far down the mountain. Far enough that the uninterrupted drop would kill him. Five-hundred years of this. Of watching his past. Of changing his present, only to discover that the infinite past lives across all six universes changed to match his new choices.

He burst out laughing, tears flowing from his eyes, his knees shaking. He howled and howled again.

The children stopped and looked down at him. His children. So it should have been.

The mother called out to them, a sweet, lily-smooth voice, pregnant with love. His wife. So it should have been.

He stood up and walked to the edge. He toed the crumbling rock and little bits of black soil fell over and into the abyss, floating out of sight. Gottverden glided among the dark clouds on the horizon, far away but giant, eclipsing his view of the universe. "Damned, damned legateurs! Damned Kamra! Damn it all!" He lifted a foot and let it hang over the abyss.

One of the yellow birds flew over and landed on his shoulder, its tiny claws puncturing his skin.

"If you go, I go."

Garbin retracted his foot and inspected the creature out of the corner of his eye. "I have truly gone mad." He laughed and moved his foot.

"The girl depends on you."

Garbin retracted his foot. "She is no longer a girl. And I am talking to a bird!"

"She is always a girl. You are always the grever. Dying will only restart your journey. You will be none the wiser but they will know your plan. They may prevent you from learning of the flaw this time."

This time?

"And the girl, she will be wiped from existence now that they have seen how helpful she is to you."

Wiped? From existence?

"So you see, Garbin. You cannot kill yourself. Continue on with Ziin's blessing."

***

"I will not change course now."

"But that weapon you told me of, wouldn't it be suicide?"

58

Supreme Leader Garbin Frigard stood on the bridge of his flagship, the *Narghorni*. He looked down on the crew at their ready stations below, crew from a thousand worlds across a million galaxies, representative of the entire universe. He looked ahead. Gottverden hung black in the sky now. Without the benefit of Verroche's atmosphere, its healthy orange hue was gone.

"Suicide is what you saved me from one thousand years ago, my dear Taka." Garbin smoothed the mop of titanium hair above his age-stained face and cleared his throat. He tapped his chest. A confirmatory beep sounded in his ear.

He'd survived the depression stage. Taka had seen to that. She was his second-in-command now. Together, they'd moved on to the remediation stage. Today would be its culmination.

"An address? Now? But that is what the device shows." Taka blinked and focused more intently on the six-screened device, now safeguarded within a lustrous podium of its own.

"Companions, our fleet stands outside the gates of the sham that is Gottverden. Its clever scheme, the proxy system, we now know was only created and perpetuated in order to bring all leaders of men, all men of initiative, to the planet of the legateurs and, once there, to grind down their independence and integrity through subornation, lack and disappearance.

"We are ten thousand warships strong. We come from all corners, peaks and valleys of this universe. We are strong and today we shall wipe Gottverden from the map. Today, you will return independence to your home worlds. No longer will it sap our best from us. No longer will we fight futile battles to right wrongs that would never be permitted to be righted. Together, we create a free universe where we may call each other brother. And where we might change our laws as we see fit, when we see fit, how we see fit and without first seeking the approval of distant legateurs.

"Today, brothers, we fight for—"

A buzzing sounded in his ear and was replaced by a voice. "Heirs of the Gottverden Sway, this is Ragfrar, Dewan of your Kamra. Your leader, Garbin Frigard, is a fraud. He once held the greatest power in the universe, the proxies of all of your worlds and even more.

"He brought this power to Gottverden. He presented his claim to the Kamra. He could have become Dewan himself. He could have overturned our one universal order then.

"But he did not. He lacked the strength and the will, just as he does now. But this time, he asks all of you to forfeit your lives to the Olindama."

Garbin tapped his chest. The beep did not sound. He looked at Taka. "Any divergence?"

She kept her eyes on the device and shook her head.

"But," Ragfrar continued, "you must also keep in mind the absurdity of his plan. We have one law, now. Your leader would reduce us to the cacophony of one-hundred million billion individual sets of law. Commerce would be destroyed as traders could not trust that a contract from one planet would be valid on another.

"Furthermore, the right of Gottverden to rule has

remained unquestioned for more than six-thousand years. There is no reason to change now. Do you not have food in your bellies? Do you not have peace in your lands? Say thank you to Gottverden. We provided that.

"Your Dewan could talk for hours about the essential need for Gottverden and about the foolishness of Garbin Frigard. But we will speak the language of your supreme leader now. Fix your eyes on his home planet of Verroche."

The command crew stood and looked out the front viewport. The green and white marble that was Verroche rolled out from behind the black planet.

They wouldn't. Verroche was their parent world, too. Destroy it and the orbit of Gottverden itself would be altered beyond all hope of redemption. They could lose their atmosphere, their...

Garbin's thoughts ran to his childhood on the peak of Mont Origl. High above the clouds, his parents raised him and his siblings. They were long gone but their bodies still rested there. Every memory of his origin was there. His fists balled at his sides. He squinted his eyes in anticipation of the blow.

"Enable viewport filters."

But the filters auto-activated before he could finish the words. A great beam of pure white flickered out from Gottverden. It hit the great ocean of Verroche and was gone.

"Was that real?" a crewman asked from below.

"It was the Olindama," another said. "And we are next. Supreme Leader, we must retreat."

A great curving fire burst out from the great ocean, flowing too fast in all directions at once. His thoughts ran to his shack, the family that lived in it back then. He should have killed himself then. Then their descendants might still be alive. Strength left his body and he sagged.

Taka's eyes remained on the device. She turned dials, magnified and reduced. The light of the device shone up at her and reflected in her eyes. She turned to him and shook her head.

A thousand years outsmarting Ziin's plan yet he wins once more.

A beam of light flickered out from Gottverden. Garbin reached for Taka. She tore the device from the podium and they ran. Behind them the ship ripped open, sliced by the Olindama, again and again.

***

"They are readying the remains of the fleet for the final battle."

"Then we will not. Send the survivors away. Disperse them to their home planets."

Taka looked up from the device. "But they are firing now and Gottverden is vaporized!" She passed the device to him.

Garbin paced the bridge of the tiny transport ship they'd found their way to after the commotion of the Olindama attack. White surfaces made the weaponless craft seem infinite. Gottverden grew in the viewport.

He received the device and watched. "What about in the last iteration?"

"The same! Victory!"

He shook his head. He'd reviewed those records dozens of times going back dozens of lifetimes. Every encounter with Gottverden ended in death. Why was this one any different? "So damned clever. I still wonder if this is a trick."

"First it shows us defeat, then it magically changes to show us victory? I don't understand it but it shows victory now. We must recall the fleet." Taka's eyes were tired. Though they were framed by deep, dry wrinkles, they were the same ones he saw more than fifteen hundred years ago when Ragfrar gave her to him, on the planet below.

But why? She was his right hand. And she was only a baby then. She was no tool of Gottverden. She was his tool, his saving force. He would never have made it this far without her.

The Olindama flickered and the beam passed by them. It flickered again. The ship shook and an alarm sounded.

"Evasive maneuvers program ansuz gebo. Merge." Garbin strode to the pilot's seat. He found the Olindama and told the ship to land him just beyond it.

The weapon flickered again, just to starboard. They entered the atmosphere. Flames licked the viewport. The ship rose and fell beneath him.

"We can still recall the fleet!" Taka grabbed his shoulder. "I am doing it now."

Garbin stood up and slapped her across the face. "No! That is the trick!" He tapped his chest. "This is Supreme

Leader Garbin Frigard. The fleet shall disperse. Return to your home planets. Divide my ships and weapons fairly amongst yourselves, as brothers. Under no circumstances may you ever return to Gottverden. Ignore any further orders."

Taka kneeled on the floor. "You must stop."

He knocked the device from her hands. It skidded across the floor and crashed into the back wall of the bridge. Dials flew off and bits of the casing spread out across the floor.

He wagged a finger in her face. "Doing the opposite of what the screen shows has served us well for fifteen hundred years. We've made it farther than in any past life. We won't stop now."

"I don't want to start over. Not again. I can't bear it, Father."

The ship zoomed towards the surface. There was the Olindama. The dock was abandoned. The doors of the receiving station opened and a mob poured forth.

He grabbed the controls. The ship slowed to a delicate float and he set it down between the Olindama and the receiving station.

"Do not cry, my dear Taka, we are breaking the chain. By ceasing to struggle, we break the chain." He stood and made for the door.

Taka threw herself across the floor and grabbed the device. Her hands shook. "There is no image..."

The door slid open. He walked down the plank to the great weapon. He stuck his hand into the opening and pulled. Nothing. He held one hundred percent of the proxies again. He commanded a grand army, the greatest ever seen. He held the loyalty of every planet in the universe. But still the Olindama resisted him.

Why?

"Father, I don't think I can fix it. I—"

The mob curved around the ship like water flowing past a rock. Dirty, soiled, teeth bared and eyes red, the masses set upon him, hands reaching, fingers scratching, teeth biting. But he was prepared.

With great kicks and twirling, impossible movements, he cut every one of them. He dusted himself off, patted dry the sweat on his brow and turned back to the ship.

"We're going to the Kamra." He strode forward and the approaching gendarmes parted to let him pass.

The steward appeared behind them and stopped in his path. "You have no invitation."

"I require none." Garbin drew his weapon from his belt and fired three shots into the steward. The man fell, laughing to the rocky ground.

He pushed through the receiving station. A vibration ran through his feet. He stopped. Windows broke and the rock opened ahead of him. He jumped over the crevasse, found the door that led to the Kamra and passed through it. He climbed the spiral staircase to the podium.

A grever received a red light and the next stepped forward to make his plea. Garbin held out a hand to stop him.

"But, it's my turn, Supreme Leader. I traveled nine years to come here. I left my family behind, a wife and three children, parents, a farm and—"

"You're a greedy fool is what you are. Do not dare approach." Garbin touched his weapon. He walked to the Dewan.

The Dewan angled his head back and narrowed his eyes. Garbin recognized the boy. He'd regrown the beard. He was a tad shorter. His visage radiated pride now, and indifference. And he wore the tall cap and long gown of the Dewan. But he was only a man.

"You dare not—" Ragfrar started.

Garbin knocked the cap off his head with a quick slap. The flimsy decoration floated to the floor. "Get the robe off, now!"

Fear took Ragfrar's eyes. He pulled the robe over his head. "What do you want me—"

Garbin knocked it from the boy's hand and the garment fluttered into the cold, dark abyss below.

"But, someone must wear the robes!" Ragfrar looked down into the darkness.

A vibration ran through the podium. It shook and Garbin steadied himself. The spotlights came to life, one after another and a cry rose from the legateurs. They ran for the exits. Dust fell from above and the grevers scurried back into the darkness.

Garbin checked his comtrer. It showed one-hundred point zero zero percent. He grinned.

"The law changes now. Rectifying the fatal flaw of which I spoke so long ago requires just one adjustment to the Gottverden order. Let us begin."

***

"Get out! Get out of my house! This is mine now!"

"Father, have we done it?"

Taka hugged him from behind. But Garbin's blood was too hot.

"Not now. Almost." He turned back to the Kamra and the fleeing legateurs. "Get out!" He looked back at Taka. "We need to empty the planet. If we can't fly them to another, we will simply push them into the abyss."

"That won't be necessary." Heavy footsteps fell on the spiral staircase.

Garbin drew his weapon and fired. The steward topped the stairs. One foot made it to the landing. Then the next. Garbin fired again. The bolts disappeared. The steward smiled up at him. He waved a hand across his face and it changed. Where there was once the mean face of humble origins, a golden, blemish-free visage shone out now.

Garbin looked at Taka. "It's Ziin!"

Ziin waved his hand at her and Taka dissolved into dust, the particles sparkling as they floated down.

Garbin knelt down and grabbed handfuls of Taka-dust, his mouth wide, his breath coming in great fits.

"The device was but a trick. The proxy system was indeed a ruse to discover men of initiative and quality. But not, as you thought, to impoverish the universe, but to safeguard it. To find the one man, the man of greatest integrity. You, Garbin." Ziin caressed the kneeling man's hair and smiled down at him.

"You must bring her back."

"She was but another trick, one that lived twenty lifetimes too many. But we are done with tricks, my dear Garbin. You may have the change you so desperately desired."

Garbin looked up at him. "But I love her."

"I am tired, you see. There is great power in the center. And it must be protected. You will protect it now as Dewan of the Kamra. And as a god. You will join the community of gods and watch over the people you care so deeply about."

But all I care about now is Taka.

Ziin waved his hand over Garbin's head and at once his youth was restored. His scraggly gray hair became silky and wheat blonde once more. The deep crags of his face receded. His muscles rebounded. His back straightened and he grew taller.

"Rise, my son, you are a god now and I name you permanent Dewan of the Kamra."

"These were all levels, weren't they?"

"Go on."

"Leaving Verroche. Refusing the bribe. Fighting on and returning." He sighed. "What is the next level to this godforsaken maze?"

"No more levels, no more tricks. Not godforsaken but god-cherished. You are among peers now. You are at the summit of the mountain once more, my son."

Once more. Garbin collapsed to the floor. Verroche. The refreshing tickle of the cool mountain air on his cheeks. The pleasant smell of the fruit trees in spring. The delicate laughs of the children. All gone.

"Why did you destroy Verroche?"

Ziin's face darkened. "Gottverden is your home planet now. A new life you are beginning. This planet is your plaything. Reform it as you see fit. But reconstitute the Kamra at the earliest possible hour. There is power in the center. We cannot stop the people from coming. Trying would be unwise. This is yours now."

He proffered a long golden key to Garbin. Garbin reached for it.

***

"And you will need to hire a new steward. May I suggest Ragfrar? The time is right for my retirement."

Garbin blinked and Ziin was gone. He flew down the spiral staircase, out of the Kamra, through the receiving station and to the Olindama.

Garbin laughed. All this power. Everything he had fought for for fifteen hundred years. And now this? He ran his finger over the keyhole in the ancient sculpture.

The sun glinted on the roof of the Kamra. In the other direction, the great line of shuttles was a thin snake in the mid-morning sky.

No. The certainty welled up in him like a powerful wave breaking over a sandbar. *No. Break the chain. Taka...*

He inserted the key into the keyhole and his hand into the opening. Metal clanged against metal deep inside the rock and the sculpture rotated freely. He gripped the cool handle and fingered the trigger. He looked back. The shuttles were still far.

Ragfrar ran out of the receiving station, naked now without the Dewan's robes. He threw himself to the ground.

Garbin swiveled the weapon towards the Kamra. He lined up the sights and pulled the trigger.

Light flickered, light brighter than any discharge of electricity, any sunburst, any engine ignition he had ever witnessed. He closed his eyes and opened them, blinking, expecting blindness.

But he was a god now.

Ragfrar lay on the ground, his limbs jerking, guttural groans rising from his throat.

The top of the Kamra, the rounded golden peak he had admired and respected so long ago — a line of flame and emptiness ran through it now.

He pushed forward on the Olindama and set its sights on the receiving station. He closed his eyes. He fired, again and again, countless times. The great light flickered until he thought the entire planet was surely gone. He opened his eyes. The Kamra, nay the city itself, was only a mound of rubble now.

He rotated the great weapon one hundred and eighty degrees. He sighted it in, closed his eyes and fired, again and again.

Hands grabbed his shoulders and pulled him backwards.

"No! You won't destroy this. You don't know what came before. They haven't told you!"

Ragfrar sat on his chest, his fists at the ready. Garbin reached up and wrapped his hand around the boy's neck. He stood up and held him high. Ragfrar wheezed and gasped, spittle flying from his mouth, his eyes bulging.

Garbin steadied his breathing. After fifteen hundred years of combat, he had grown strong. But this kind of strength, this could only be granted by the gods. He walked over to the edge of the abyss, next to the great press. Ragfrar's feet dangled into the darkness.

The boy looked down. "You can't do this."

Garbin let go. "I just did."

He turned back to the Olindama. Shuttles began to land. Their doors slid open but the grevers waited.

Garbin trained the sights of the great weapon on the first shuttle. "Return to your homes. Never come back. Or die."

One man stepped from the third shuttle. His blonde hair was a careless mop. His sturdy shoulders and strong cheekbones projected a desultory confidence. "Dewan, I have discovered a fatal flaw in the law that must be rectified."

Garbin trained the weapon on the man. *Is it restarting? Why does he look like me?* He poked his head out. "You refer to the issue of consent?"

The grevers crowded the shuttle exits but no other dared venture forth.

The man's face brightened. "Yes, indeed. There was never a grant of—"

"Stop!" Garbin yelled.

The grevers recoiled. The man narrowed his eyes.

"I only wish to be heard."

"I brought the same grievance here fifteen hundred years ago.

Today, I myself am answering it. The flaw is remedied. The Kamra is dissolved. Return to your homeworlds. Send forth no more grevers. Gottverden is dead. Rule yourselves. Make your own laws. Go in peace, trade in peace and let each man choose for himself his path through life, without interference from far-off legateurs, other order-givers, the gods or even Ziin himself. Now go!"

The man stepped forward. "But what of you?"

"My place is here. I will watch over the center of power. No one will use it again."

The man stepped forward. "Alone? Here? No, you will need help."

Garbin trained the sights and fired. A chunk of rock at the man's feet disappeared, replaced by the blackness of the abyss below.

"You will all leave now. Never come back. When honor is in question, remember me and let my fate empower your hearts to find the strength to stand up for that which is right and good. Now go!"

George Donnelly is the author of space opera, robot apocalypse and dystopian science fiction series. A rebel and unreformed idealist, he believes equally in human rights and abundant hugs before bedtime. Get a new free short story every month at georgedonnelly.com.

The Vote
by Allan Davis

Only four more calls today, Vincent thought, *and I can go home.*

He checked the screen, pulling up the next name on his list, adjusted the headset, and waited for the call to go through. He took a deep, relaxing breath while the line rang, once, twice, and then was answered partway through the third. The audio light on the screen lit up, flickering in time with the syllables coming from the far end of the connection.

With a well-practiced air, Vincent went into his script. "Good evening, Mr. MacKenzie. My name is Vincent, and I work for the SG Group, which has been contracted by the government to carry out the…"

The man's irate voice cut into his perfectly prepared speech, but Vincent refused to let it rattle him. "Yes, sir, that's correct, that's exactly what I'm calling about. That makes this much easier since you already—"

Vincent winced and closed his eyes at the blast of offensive words that came streaming through the headset.

He reached out and clicked the Mute button, saving his ears from the assault, and waited for the audio light to go back out before returning the volume to normal.

"I'm sorry you feel that way, sir, really, but I'm just doing my job here. The law is the law, and—"

He waited patiently for MacKenzie to run out of steam again, and was actually reaching for the mute button again when the man finally went quiet again. "No, Mr. MacKenzie, it's not my job to decide the merits of the law; it's my job to carry it out. Now, I need to let you know that…"

For the second time, Vincent clicked off the sound, and waited patiently for the light to flicker out again. He rubbed the bridge of his nose between thumb and forefinger. *Why do they have to argue so much?* he thought.

"Mr. MacKenzie, yes, I know, it does seem terribly unfair. But believe me, we—"

He took another slow, deep breath, but the level of offensiveness and also the volume were steadily dropping. Vincent appreciated that; after three times on mute, he was permitted to drop the call and hand the situation over to local law enforcement, and that was so much harder all the way around. Better to get them to listen to reason.

"Look, sir, the law was submitted, voted on, and properly passed in a nationwide vote. I'm sure you heard about it, and if you didn't like it, you should have voted against—"

For the third time, Vincent hit the mute button. He would be within regulations to terminate this call at any time, but he decided to try to stick it out.

"Well, then, sir, you have absolutely nothing to complain about! If you could not even be bothered to vote on what was quite possibly the most important poll in history, then you have no one to blame but yourself."

There was angry spluttering on the other end of the line, but Vincent was on a roll now, and refused to let it even slow him down.

"The law was passed. 51% voted in favor. That's a majority. That's democracy in action. Fifty one percent of the population agreed that it was necessary—and accepted, and legal—to eat the remaining forty-nine percent."

He took just enough of a breath to continue. "Now, I regret to inform you that your number has come up in the draft. It is your civic responsibility to follow the law. You therefore have seventy-two hours to report to the nearest available SG Soylent facility for processing. Good day, sir."

He closed the channel, tore off the headset, and dropped it on the desk in front of him. *Stubborn old fools, thinking they know the law better than the government. Who the heck do they think they are?*

He shuffled around the office, refilling his coffee cup before moving on to the three remaining calls. The nature of his position didn't bother him all that much; he was, of course, simply doing his job. And, as such, he knew that his own position was secure. As part of the SG group, he was automatically part of the 51%.

He settled down into his cubicle again, adjusting his headset, and was just about to dial the next number when the phone rang. The unfamiliar noise made him jump, and he reached out to answer before it could ring a second time. This phone never rang. This was an outgoing line only. "Hello...?"

"Hello, Vincent Garza? My name is Blake, and I've been contracted by the SG Group to call you and tell you that your number has come up in the draft..."

By day, Allan is a mild-mannered computer geek. But by night...he creates worlds so the other people who live in his mind have somewhere to play. Science fiction, fantasy, and horror spew out of the dark and twisted corners of his brain, with political rants or humorous work thrown in just to keep people guessing. Never, under any circumstances, allow him to sing after midnight. Or before midnight. Find his works at allandavisjr.blogspot.com.

One Small Step for Mein Führer
by Alex R. Knight III

The LEM had landed just a short time ago, and Handel now planted the swastika pennant into the lunar soil.

Over the crests of deceivingly distant gray mountains, he could see the lone blue marble of Earth. Beyond that, only the black and empty void stretching off to the impossibly distant stars — dozens, hundreds, thousands of light years away.

He admired the flag for a moment, the way steel wires held it in billowing furls, as though it were waving even here in the vacuum of space. He stretched his right arm out in salute for the MESA camera, a stillshot for the ages, one for all the *volk* to watch on television and look at in the history books for years to come.

After a respectful length, Handel bounded his way back towards the capsule, leaving behind bootprints in the powdery, ashen soil that would still be there millennia from now. The thought both humbled and fascinated him. He was a member of a superior breed, true enough, and an *übermensch* among even them to have come this far, but still: The Führer's Thousand Year Reich, though victorious enough to have subdued both the English and the Russians, would not last forever. To give voice to such a historical inevitability – though its essential truth was openly admitted in the very title the Führer himself had lent it – was treason in the highest, of course. But Handel had nonetheless determined to hold on to it for as long as he might. Better *Deutschland,* the Fatherland, than America with its cesspool of Negroes and plutocracy of Jews.

He reached the foot of the ladder. There was a plaque attached to the framework of the LEM's landing gear — apparatus that would remain behind when Handel returned to Earth.

ON JULY 21, 1969, A RACIALLY PURE GERMAN LANDED HERE.
HE CAME IN PEACE AND BROTHERHOOD FOR ALL ARYAN-KIND.
LONG LIVE THE GERMAN REICH!
LONG LIVE THE FÜHRER!

It was nearly time, in fact, to speak with the Führer. If only Herr Hitler himself had lived to see this! He took hold of the first rung, and started pulling himself with reduced-gravitational ease up the side of the sleek, glossy black capsule. The scarlet, ivory, and ebony insignia of the Reich stood out in bold livery. It would in fact aid the *kriegsmarine* in pinpointing the capsule after he made splashdown in the North Atlantic just three or four days from now.

A spike of pain shot through his right shoulder with violent, piercing intensity, and he howled inside the thick fishbowl of his helmet. Berlin had just enough time to ask him if anything was wrong before *Mond-Astronauten* Handel Eckart let tear another such — this one even more wild, lengthier, and entirely unrestrained. Back at the New Chancellery, the blood of an entire roomful of *Missions Kontrolle* personnel had a slush of hoarfrost dumped into it.

It dwarfed the LEM as an elephant might tower over a small Volkswagen. It too wore a pressure suit — though one of very different design. Six tentacleish arms protruded from its hulking torso like branches. Two of these now had Handel in the clutch of their crab-like claws; pincers that may or may not have been mechanically assisted, but which, either way, were more savagely strong than a pair of vises. A quadruple set of bloated purple eyes glared at Handel from behind a tinted visor, carrying in themselves all the emotional depth of an insect. The dark pupils flared dispassionately. Handel watched the creature open its salivating jaws inside the helmet sphere, revealing rows of razor fangs large as dragon's teeth. Its skin was a leprous, warty brown. Handel went mute then, frozen with shock and complete terror even as Berlin hailed him frantically for a response of any kind.

One corner of his bugging eyes caught the ambiguous wink and gleam of a silvery metallic object some guiling distance away near a mountain. It shimmered on the lunar surface as if it were some desert mirage. Coming towards him from it were three more such monstrosities. They trundled towards the landing site with an alacrity that made utterance of whatever their strange language might be superfluous. Handel knew what he was to them well enough. Analysis. An experiment.

Food.

They reduced the LEM to wreckage – its twisted remains neutralized in the midst of all the grand lunar desolation. The last sound anyone at the New Chancellery heard before cutoff was Handel Eckart venting a scream of such desperate and high-pitched horror that everyone on up to the Führer was left to probe its nuances over and over, making hypothetical guesses as to the basis of its origin and ultimate meaning. Several generations of subsequent scientists and researchers would do the same, in fact, for years and years to come.

Following this terrible catharsis, *Mond-Astronauten* Eckart's capacity for both fear and pain elapsed rather quickly. Consciousness drifted away from him like helium escaping from a ruptured balloon.

The others, anticipating only a brief stopover, returned to their vehicle with a new and unexpected prize.

Ein Proben. Nein Ubermenschen.

Alex R. Knight III is originally from Groveland, Massachusetts, where he grew up listening to rock and roll, reading J.R.R. Tolkien, and the comic books of the 1970s. He today lives in rural southern Vermont where he welds, plays guitar, paints abstracts, reads avidly, and writes. He is the author of the short fiction collection Tales From Dark 7, *in addition to the novels* The Morris Room *and* Empty World. *And, he is a Voluntaryist. Find his works at his Facebook page.*

The Thing on the Nightstand
by Allan Davis

You voted today.

You threw your weight into the gun control debate by helping to choose the candidate and the law, stayed up a bit late celebrating the victory, and finally crawled into bed. And as you doze off, you reach over and pat the thing on the nightstand, making sure it's ready if you need it.

Around 4:00AM, something—you're not quite sure what—jolts you awake. You lie there, staring at the ceiling, wondering what it was, when you hear it again…a noise, downstairs, like someone walking around the living room. And now that noise—that was the sound of someone opening a drawer and searching through it. There's a thief downstairs, going through your stuff, looking for something of value. Isn't that why you keep the thing on the nightstand?

You reach over, remembering precisely where it was, but forget that there's a glass of water on the nightstand; you left that there in case you needed it also. In the dark, your searching hand knocks the glass off onto the floor.

All noise from downstairs stops…and then you hear the unmistakable noise of feet on stairs. Wasn't that the creaky fifth step?

There, you've found it, it's in your hand, you're ready now. Just in time, too; the feet have reached the top of the stairs, and your bedroom door slowly swings open. There's a man standing there, with wild greasy hair, red watery eyes, and a gun held in a shaky hand, and because it's pointed at you, the barrel looks like it's three feet across. Even from across the room, you can smell a week's worth of sweat and alcohol. His eyes are darting around the room, checking to make sure no one else is there.

Ah, but you're ready for him, and doing exactly what a good citizen should do in a situation like this. That's why you voted the way you did, after all. You hold up the thing from the nightstand, and it makes a noise that shatters the silence and causes both of you to jump.

From it, a tinny, quiet voice says, "911, what's the emergency?"

By day, Allan is a mild-mannered computer geek. But by night…he creates worlds so the other people who live in his mind have somewhere to play. Science fiction, fantasy, and horror spew out of the dark and twisted corners of his brain, with political rants or humorous work thrown in just to keep people guessing. Never, under any circumstances, allow him to sing after midnight. Or before midnight. Find his works at allandavisjr.blogspot.com.

The Flight of New China: Spaceship Pingdeng
by Wallace Runnymede

Rat-a-tat-tat.

Such a sound.

Reminiscent of the grand old China our ancestors once remembered; but even they were too old to live there.

Of course, in that old society, they were not equal.

***

There were boundaries.

There were the five and three.

Bonds of social belonging, bonds of responsibility.

Or was it the other way round?

Five and three, five and three.

We no longer know how to count backwards…

Did we ever?

We must do.

Their boundary was society.

But it was also the planet earth.

***

We dreamed that if only we could escape this barren planet after the May 5 incident, it would not be difficult to explore the boundless reaches of the Kosmos, as dreamed our most exalted visionary, Kang Youwei. He spoke of a 'Great Sameness,' a 'Grand Community of Perfect Equality.'

Some said it was at the cost of liberty.

But then again, the gloomy, unconstructively pessimistic novelist, Lao She, wrote his idle dystopia 'The City of Cats.' By reducing our proud nation to squabbling felines, he denied that the outer reaches of the Universe were ours to explore.

***

So on the one hand, we, yes we, the New Chinese, have crossed every galaxy in search of a new age. The old ways weren't working any longer; neither our ways, nor those of our fellow-planeteers.

We sought wisdom within a narrow sphere; but this was no use for us.

The prison-cage of the feudal clan became the prison cage of the world.

We could not rest easy, we could not ever be satisfied.

Liberalism and Communism alike were of our world.

We wanted a Greater Good even than these.

***

After May 5, the hacking of the Global Geo-Engineering complex left us no choice but to leave this planet, before our enemies finished us off.

But why speak more? For is there not an old Occidental proverb (if my memory does not betray me), that, 'the man who roars in space shall never get a hearing.'

Or was it our Confucius?

It is also said that Confucius was of the bones of long-dead men.

Once upon a time, it was said that, 'China needs fewer - isms, and has need only of this: our practicality.'

There once was a time that 'liberty' was a word fresh and new.

But we are uprooted from that word by now.

And why?

Because those who treasured liberty, among us and afar from us, traded freedom for a sturdy seat on Spaceship Earth.

***

We used to say that Liberty is a lifeboat; the only way to avoid capsizing it, is to steady your own ship.

This was our truth...

But it became our lie.

We never dreamed the May 5 incident would destroy all life on Earth.

Why were we the ones that were spared?

Now freedom, this treasure of the human race, is

committed into our hands alone.

. . .

Would to Heaven we knew what to do with it!

Wallace Runnymede is a progressive/left-liberal who has strongly libertarian views on freedom of speech, non-interventionism and privacy. Aside from his blog Wallace Runnymede, *he also runs the website* Satire Catastrophes. *With the assistance of Appleseed Ike, he runs the* Peace Criminals Website Trilogy, *a collection of centrist websites for pacifists and non-interventionists:* Neocon Surveillance, Neocon Surveillance Network, *and the* Satirical-Industrial Complex.

Escape from the Keep
by Heather Biedermann

There are moments in life where you know you have just made a terrible mistake. My screaming "Fuck the government!" into the face of a Silver Shield Enforcer was probably not the best of choices made this week.

Growing up in Silver City, I learned to avoid fights and find peaceful ways of resolving conflict. This Enforcer had stopped me because I jaywalked and he was bored. Being in a hurry, I was impatient and gave him a little attitude. Things escalated quickly. About to get arrested for this stupid crime, I started swearing and mocking the "useless government." In retrospect, I probably should have kept my mouth shut.

A powerful fist flew through the air and made contact with my face right after the words left my mouth. Silver Shield police wear grey, lightweight armor in the field. Their silver, reflective helmets make it impossible to see the officer's eyes under their masks. I could only see the smirk of his mouth to know that he was definitely in the mood to fight. On his chest plate, you could see a shiny silver badge embossed into the armor with the name "Richards" and his badge number. Another punch and I felt shadows starting to fill my eyes as I flew backward to the ground.

I pulled myself up with newfound determination. Flicking my long blonde hair out of my eyes, I spat a mouthful of blood right onto his chin. I looked down at my favorite black t-shirt, which now had a gaping rip across the front revealing a peek of bra and white, blood-splattered skin underneath. "Damn it, I liked that shirt," I growled.

Jumping up, I kicked the enforcer in the side of the knee, which gave an audible crunch. He predictably tipped over to his side, the heavy armor throwing him off balance, and the stun baton he was swinging to use on me went flying.

Here is the thing — he wasn't wrong about stopping me. I had actually just robbed the jewelry store nearby. It is what I do. Normally, I'm not so messy about things like that, but my girlfriend Delilah's birthday is today. I should have been in and out, like a normal job. This time, I had no backup. I was sloppy and in a hurry. To be caught because I jaywalked is almost too much for me to bear.

I had found the perfect necklace for my girlfriend — a one-of-a-kind red ruby and diamond necklace just like one that purple-eyed famous actress once owned so long ago. A necklace so lovely, it really had no business even being in a jewelry store in such a dismal shit-pile like Silver City. But who am I to question destiny?

The necklace reminded me of lazy days snuggling on the overstuffed blue velvet couch in Delilah's apartment watching those ancient movies on her holoprojector. She loved the old shows with classy dames dripping with jewels and how everything seemed to be in slow motion. Delilah would straighten her shoulder length black hair into a wavy bob, put on bright red lipstick, and shimmy into a skintight dress. She looked like a knockout. I told her she was the "black bombshell," and she would throw her arms around my neck and shower me with kisses. Those were the best days, before we were trying to make ends meet by pulling the odd burglary jobs here and there.

In the distance, I could hear the chiming of a church tower. It must be seven. I was going to be late for our dinner date together. I eyed my bag that had the necklace in it and reached down to grab it. Inside was a clear plastic drive that was used to exchange coin. It was the method of choice for paying off police and the sort. No getting around this city easily without greasing the wheels sometimes. It usually worked, as most of the Enforcers were pretty open to being paid off. I guess it probably has something to do with them wanting to avoid paperwork and feeling underappreciated on the state's dime.

"Officer Richards," I pleaded. "We may have gotten off on the wrong foot. You think I'm someone I'm not. I thought you were just trying to hurt me and I got scared." I did my best weak, innocent little-girl act. This is where I can tell if they are about to soften up, but the Enforcer didn't waiver.

Still, I went on, "I know how hard you all work, and I'd like to give you a donation to help rein in the criminal element of Silver City." I held out the clear plastic transfer drive. "60,000 units help the cause?" Usually, this was more than enough to get a nod and a goodbye.

Richards' head turned to look at the bribe. He paused a moment and looked up coldly at me. "I don't want your money," he growled suddenly. "You are going to prison for sedition, treason, and assaulting an officer of the law. And now attempting to bribe an officer. You are judged guilty, and you will be going straight to the Keep."

"Don't forget jaywalking," I grinned at him. I knew right when I said it, that it was a mistake.

He took off his helmet, and it showed that he had a head of shaved gray hair and placed the helmet on the seat of his hover cycle. I could see his black eyes filled with cold hate. "I'm going to make an example of you. But first…I'm going to hurt you," his pale face twisted into a horrible smile.

With that, he lunged forward at me. He swung the baton, hitting my head and arms. I rolled out of the way, ducking to get out of his reach. His boot kicked at my belly and connected. I flew through the air, my slender body flying back against a garbage can. My hand found a long metal pipe jutting out of the can, and I pulled it out and swung wildly at the policeman. The metal met its target with a wet clang, but as it hit, I was surprised to see a couple of screws sticking out of the end of my weapon. I dropped the pipe, and stared as it hung in the place where it had connected with his head. Blood dripped from his forehead and into his eyes.

Officer Richards stood still for a moment, his hand reaching up to touch at the nails going deep into his head.

His eyes rolled back, and he fell to his side.

"Shit." I said, "I can't kill a cop," I thought to myself. He must have already scanned my info into the system. I reached to pick up my bag and got ready to run. I thought maybe I could pick up Delilah and get out of town fast.

A shiny black police vehicle silently pulled up next to me in the alley. The side door slid open. Two slim droids with glowing blue and red flashing eyes hopped out.

"Tilde Harris — you are under arrest. Your rights are forfeit as a lawbreaker deemed guilty by an Enforcer of Silver City. Do not resist," the droid calmly stated right as it used a stun pulse on me. Everything faded to black.

***

My head was throbbing. Something smelled so bad I couldn't even stand it. I hope that isn't me. I was in a humming electric vehicle and slowly opened my eyes. My hands were cuffed behind my back and fastened to the gray plastic seat. I looked around and saw I was on a bus loaded with women.

I heard sobbing around the bus. "I didn't do anything," an elderly, tiny black woman repeated.

"Shut the hell up, Grandma," a chubby, pink-haired girl said as she kicked at the crying woman.

My eyes scanned over the clean bus filled with women. A thin droid walked up and down the aisle eyeing the passengers. At the front of the bus, behind a cage was another droid driving the rig and next to it was the only human Enforcer, a broad-shouldered female officer wearing the silver armor and brandishing a huge rifle.

I could see out the slim strip of windows on the sides of the bus that we were just pulling into the first gates of a large government building. It was the district's mega prison called the Keep. The prison was brightly lit, and the whole outside of the huge skyscraper was covered in a holographic projection surface. An advertisement played of a young brunette prisoner drinking the popular Ambrosia Cola. The 3D image of the woman thrusted out the drink towards the audience approaching on the bus, and I instinctively ducked away from the bottle.

"Must be the corporate sponsor," I mumbled aloud. The droid in the aisle made a clicking sound at me and I remembered where I was.

Up until this point in my life, I never had even come close to landing in a prison. Before today, I was convinced only dumb criminals or poor, unfortunate people ended up here.

We all heard the stories about how the prisons were overflowing, much like the other prisons in the region. In the last fifty years, the legal system had become so overwhelmed, that it was decided to give the power of sentencing to the Enforcers. If a decision was thought to be unjust, a person could ask for a hearing in the court system. However, the courts were so completely overloaded, that it usually would take about 5 to 10 years to even meet with your counselor, much less even start your case. The best defense was to not even end up here if you could help it.

Bribery was the best way to stay out of jail, and as long as you were rich, you pretty much wouldn't end up here. Well, here I was.

The building was getting closer, and I noticed that we drove over a bridge. I could see a massive gate coming up ahead, and a sign across the top that read "Welcome to the Keep. Visitors and residents to Gate A. Inmates to Gate B. Employees and Vendors to Gate C."

The video ceiling of the bus suddenly came alive with a chipper-voiced woman. "Welcome to your new home, Prison Colony 4-2-K, commonly known as the Keep." The words seemed to float away as she continued. "The Keep follows the philosophy of rewarding hard work and teamwork within the community as a path to redemption. Those that follow the rules and obey will have a comfortable life here. Those that break the rules will be punished accordingly."

"Inmates have many choices on their path to redemption. You can work a job to earn credits that can help you pay for all the comforts of home. You can benefit from the free educational programs offered. With good behavior and enough credits, you can even arrange to be moved to one of our low-security floors where you can choose to have outside family live together with you. We will even help you train to see if you have what it takes to be an Enforcer yourself when your stay is over."

They make it sound like we are on some sort of holiday, I thought. Before I could even start to rant, the door to the bus opened and the lock around my handcuffs released. All the women rose to their feet and shuffled off the bus to be processed.

***

"Tilde Evelyn Harris," said a crisp female voice as I approached a huge glowing screen. On the left, my name appeared and my citizen identification code. My smiling photograph was next to it. A list of my minor infractions filled the screen, but then the screen faded. "You are sentenced for jaywalking, sedition, treason, grand larceny, disturbing the peace, assault, battery and murder of an Enforcer. Your sentence is life pending your trial if you should choose to pursue one. Please answer yes or no — Would you like a trial for these crimes?"

I sat stunned and was just processing the fact that I was definitely in prison and definitely didn't want to be here. "Repeating the question, would you…," the voice said again slowly. "Yes, goddamn it. Of course I want a trial."

"Very well," the voice continued, "you are now added to the list of those requesting a public defender. The wait list for a counselor is estimated at approximately ten years."

I knew this was coming, but it still felt like a punch to the gut.

The voice continued, "If you can afford a private defender, this time may be reduced down to five years. Or if you participate in the Keep's weekly lottery, you could find yourself the winner of the services of a star lawyer!" The screen filled with glittering stars as the faces of celebrity lawyers from popular court television shows swirled around. A disclaimer whispered off to the side that she could barely hear — something about donating credits to the lottery does not mean you will win the lottery. I disgustedly shook my head.

My feet were on a moving walkway, and I slowly was transported down a brightly lit passage. On both sides were more screens showing a procession of Ambrosia Cola advertisements, mixed with the information about my "stay."

I hope I could see my girlfriend soon. She is going to be so pissed at me, and they won't let anyone make calls for 24 hours during our processing. Maybe she will have an idea on how to get me out of this place?

Robotic arms came out of the walls, and a light scanned me. A mist of tiny bug-like creatures swarmed up from the ground and my bloody clothing disappeared. "Freaking nanobots," I thought as I was stripped nude. Those little robots pretty much got rid of everything on me, and also stitched up all the cuts and lacerations.

I had heard horror stories of the nanos growing extra arms on people accidentally. I tried not to think about it, although an extra arm might come in handy for stealing things and in giving fantastic hand jobs. I stifled my giggle at that thought.

It crossed my mind that there had been debates on the news about using the nanos to correct "unpatriotic behavior" in prisoners. The tests on subjects had been unsuccessful, whatever that meant. Maybe their brains melted? I wondered what kind of horrible things they had in mind for prisoners like me.

The nanos started to sew a new outfit — the light blue jumpsuit of the inmates of the Keep. This had my name in black across the front with my new ID number and a photo of myself sewn into the material. I readied myself as I could see the end of the walkway was approaching. I walked out into what almost looked like a shopping mall dotted with robotic guards. A fake sunny sky was projected overhead, and the canned sounds of birds and nature were all around me. People were milling about in the area, and I heard someone call out my name.

"Tilde! Holy shit, is that you?" a thin, smiling black woman with short blue hair came running out of the crowd. She had the same blue jumpsuit on, but over the top, she had colorful little braids of fabric tied to make a fringe around her waist. She wore a pink backpack that was covered in stickers of videogame characters and computer logos. Relief filled me when I recognized her as my favorite lady nerd, Denise Schulz.

***

"Schulz," I said, "What the hell are you doing in here?" She pulled me over to a bench under a tree.

"Well, I got ratted out for hacking. Son-of-a-bitch Robbie threw me under the bus."

I shook my head in disappointment, "Yeah, that Robbie was a creep. Sorry to hear it. But at least it's nice to see your friendly face in here." We traded stories of what happened since the last time we saw each other. We had been pretty good friends before I had started dating Delilah. I guess sometimes friendships fade when you start an intense relationship.

"Honestly, Tilde," she said lowering her voice to a whisper, "I've learned so much in here. My skills are so much better now than when I was on the outside." She leaned closer and said, "You got here at just the right time. Something big is going down. We can't talk about it here, but I'll help get you checked into your room and tell you everything."

***

"Most of the people that come here will never leave again," Schulz started. We sat in her tiny one-room apartment. The room was tidy, with a painting of flowers on the wall. A twin bed and a low-end holoprojector were against the far wall. I sat at the small metal kitchen table across from her.

"They design it so you get here and are comfortable. You do jobs for them so you think you have control. They even pay you some credits so you can give them right back to them for buying crappy stuff to make a nest here. Some people take their chances on putting credits into the prison lottery to win a good lawyer to get out. Really, nobody around here has ever won that."

She continued, "And if you behave yourself, you can get one of the family level apartments and have them stay here with you. Why anyone would want their kids to grow up in this prison is beyond me, but when the government pays for everything, people do it," she said.

"It really makes it easy for the system to indoctrinate children when they grow up here. Later, most of them either end up working for the government or getting arrested and living here anyways."

I shook my head and asked, "Doesn't it cost a lot to keep us here? I mean, why make things so nice?"

She said, "It is cheaper to keep us in prisons than to try to subsidize us in the real world. Here they can at least control us. Make money off of us. Out there we are in the wild. Out there, we are dangerous."

"So, you told me that something big was going on?" I asked.

Schulz nodded and leaned in, as if she was still worried someone might hear. "I've been working with a group on a way to get out. We have a plan to escape. Did you know that there are only a handful of human guards that run the Keep? Thousands of droids take care of the prisoners, but what if we could just turn them off?" she leaned back and smiled.

"Do you have a way to do that?" I asked.

She grinned even wider. "Have you ever heard of EMPs?"

"Yeah, I think so," I said. "Like those electrical pulses that kill computers?"

She nodded. "Well, the droids and the server for the system are protected against that, but we found that there is a similar way to use the charging stations that they all walk over to recharge each day to sabotage them. It really is simple. I found that you can overload the wireless magnetic resonance frequency using a device I built so it confuses the processors of the droids. They basically have a fault within them that thinks they have had too much charging and shut down into a sleep mode."

"At that point, we found that there is a weakness in their programs that make it so we can introduce an ongoing energy loop. They stay in rest mode infinitely, or at least until we tell them to wake up." She smiled. "In that time, we use one of the sleeping droids as a Trojan horse to hack the system software to open all the doors and to open the gates. Then we crash the main system program down into a sleep loop so nobody can turn it back on."

She pulled her pink backpack out and unzipped it. She pulled out a small rectangular device with silver buttons and an antenna. "There are ten of these. Not everyone who is locked at the Keep wants to leave. The brainwashing goes far and is deep. They make people want to stay here." She paused and sadly shook her head.

"It is all lies. Those that fight openly, disappear from here. Others who are caught inciting disobedience are sent to the psych wards where they mess you up with their drugs. Too many good people have fallen apart and through the cracks here," she said. "Still, we need to keep it quiet so the guards aren't tipped off to what we are up to. I trust you with this. It is our one chance of getting out of here."

"I'm with you," I said without any hesitation. "Even gilded cages are cages. I want to go home."

***

Schulz pressed the button and looked up at me. It was done. I looked around the corner and saw that the color of the droids' eyes changed from bright white to flat gray. They were in power-down mode.

"Let's go," I said, picking up my bag of gear as we signaled the growing crowd near the fountain. Schulz climbed up the concrete side of the fountain, and she threw her arms in the air. "The droids are off. The doors are open. Everyone grab guns off the droid stands and run out of the different exits. There will be opposition, but we have to try. True freedom is not under lock and key. True freedom is working together against oppression. Together we can overthrow this corrupt system. Now fly!"

The prisoners scattered like a splash in opposite directions. I ran with Schulz to the nearest guard station. The door easily opened, and I carefully slid past a dozing droid guard. I handed laser guns out to women near me. I looked carefully for the safety on the one I grabbed. I never had needed to use a gun before, and realized that there wasn't time to have anyone show me. It seemed simple enough, with a button that opened up the barrel at the same time as the safety was turned off.

We continued running towards the main gate doorway. I saw our first human enforcers near the exit. They fired laser shots at us and we ducked behind a snack cart. I shot back, hitting one of the guards in the leg and knocking him down. There was no time to feel remorse for this. We just had to push on. I could see another group further up swarming on top of the desperately firing guards, engulfing them.

A crowd of women ripped the armor off a howling female guard. I saw bits of hair flung past me, but I made myself ignore it as we ran out the door. The huge gate was wide open, and prisoners were funneling out of the darkened building.

I saw a small enforcer vehicle with a dead guard next to it. "Help me pick him up and throw him in the vehicle," I shouted. The Enforcers usually had electronic keys in their uniforms for their vehicles. It was worth a try to see if we could steal the ride.

We tossed the bloody body in the backseat. I jumped into the driver's seat, and Schulz was on the passenger side. I pushed the power button, and it whirred up. "Welcome, Officer Larmat. The system is offline, so you will need to use manual mode." The wheel popped out, and I grabbed it tight. I slammed on the accelerator pedal to take off.

We wove around groups of prisoners fighting guards on the bridge exiting the Keep. Flashes of gunfire bounced off our armored vehicle, shaking it a bit. Prisoners threw chunks of burning metal at us, not knowing we were also one of them.

Schulz sunk down in the seat next to me shaking. "This is really happening!" she exclaimed.

The huge robotic turrets sat flaccidly on the gates. Hundreds of robot guards were dormant and quiet. We drove right through the silent army of metal men. Just as we were pulling through the gates, a huge tiltwing airship flew over the Keep. I expected to see soldiers dropping down, but instead a large cylinder was dropped, and the airship took off, breaking the sound barrier with a clap.

"Is that a bomb?" I asked Schulz whose eyes grew big with the realization. A bright light went off but no explosion. "Drive! Drive!" she pleaded to me, and I pushed the car as fast as it would go. I watched in my rearview mirror. Dancing in the air wasn't fire, but what looked to be swarms of bugs. The guards at the gate ran away from the Keep in the direction of the road. I saw them get swallowed up by the bugs and just stop running like they had been switched off. They disappeared in the fog of bugs as we drove on.

"Do you think those are nanos?" I asked. "They have to be," Schulz whimpered, "Why would they use them on a prison break?" She asked. "What do you think they do to us?" I asked.

Schulz shook her head. "Oh, hell no. I don't want to find out. We've got to get away from that." Her voice trembled.

A metal wall popped up in the middle of the road. "Where the hell did that come from?" I yelled and slammed on the breaks. The car skidded sideways and slammed into the wall. The inside of the car filled with a foam that padded everything. In about 5 seconds it turned into a gas, and evaporated from the cabin.

I reached over and shook Schulz. "We have got to go," I said as I looked into her eyes to make sure she was conscious.

She nodded and opened her door to get out. My door was blocked by the wall so I slid out on her side of the vehicle and looked cautiously around as I got out. I pointed my gun up at the wall, half expecting someone to start shooting at us. Out of the corner of my eye, I could see the cloud of nanos coming upon us.

"We have to climb it," I said while pointing at the rough middle edge. There was a lip on it that looked like something you could grab if you jumped from the hood of the vehicle. I climbed on top of the car, and pulled Schulz up with me.

"We can do this." I nodded at her. I backed up and took off towards the wall with a jump. I grabbed the tiny ledge and pulled myself up. I looked around quickly and saw no one on the other side, so if we could just get over, we should be safe for now.

I kneeled down and said, "Now you. I'll try to pull you up."

I looked and behind her, I saw the nanos were fast approaching. "Come on!" I yelled.

She backed up and did a quick run to jump. Right when she was about to jump, her toe caught on the hood of the car and she fell forward, hitting her head on the wall.

"No!" I cried out still holding my hand out to her. She stood up and touched her hand to her head, blood dripping down.

"Go," she said, looking up at me as the nanos started to swarm around her. "You have to tell people what they are doing. Get out of here."

I screamed in horror as I saw her eyes change from pain to nothing. She stood motionless for a moment. Then she slowly turned around and started to walk back to the Keep.

The nanos reached the wall and began to fade like burnt ashes in the air. The commotion was over and silence blanketed the cool night air. I climbed down the other side of the wall and started my walk back to Silver City.

Heather Biedermann is a viking libertarian, librarian and a Libra. Say that five times fast! She has a masters degree in both library information science and in educational leadership. Heather lives in Minnesota with her family where she wrangles two rescue cats and is an avid fan of all things nerdy. For fun, you can find her frequenting sci-fi conventions, glamping or with her nose in a book. Find her works at heatherbiedermann.com.

The Ballad of Mama Leche
by Richard Walsh

Alexandra Souza had never wanted offspring. The whole process of coupling, birthing, child-rearing; it all smacked of patriarchy.

She'd learned about patriarchy in her third semester at the university.

During her fourth semester she read a pamphlet about the scourge of formula-feeding. "Breast is best," it said, and, even though motherhood was a concept likely advanced by corporate oligarchs, Alex was outraged that some parents chose a synthetic substitute to mother's milk.

"Formula is child abuse," read another pamphlet, this one published by a heroic, dynamic militant named Mama Leche, who wrote the tracts from a secret location and deployed platoons of her followers to the factories where the wicked formula was brewed.

Local authorities, cowed by the righteousness and fervor of the *lecheros*, did not intervene when the vigilantes dismantled stills and conveyor belts and boilers. Factory floors were left in ruins by Mama Leche's troops.

Alex enthusiastically participated. She recruited others from her classes at university and was soon given the beret of a *lechero* lieutenant. She tracked the street price of formula, pleased to see it rise week after week.

They gathered daily at a community center to hear Mama Leche speak: she radioed in, her alto voice melodic and modulated and ecstatic. Every word was a command. Every sentence a warning. Every message a prophecy.

Mama Leche informed them of shipments of formula inbound from outside of the city. *Lecheros* sang her hymn as they intercepted the trucks and dumped the poison down drains. "Nature nature, we fight for nature," they sang.

Mama Leche directed them to a black market factory. They sang her ballad as they ripped apart its machinery.

Mama Leche preached that the rising price would open women's eyes. "All they need has been given to them by nature." Financial pressure would turn babies back to the breast.

But for every factory the *lecheros* destroyed, for every tanker they overturned, for every store shelf they ripped from the wall, formula was still available to parents on the black market. Astronomically expensive, but still available, and the profits earned by the suppliers and smugglers enraged Alex further.

She stopped attending classes and instead turned to hunting. She noted that one crafty supplier consistently slipped through the blockade, continued to produce formula in the city and distribute it for profit. *Sunrise Milk*, it was called, the name a wicked attempt to deceive women and corrupt their children.

Her informants, the ones who supplied her street prices, would not give her the source of *Sunrise Milk*, so she masqueraded as a new mother, cowed by the weight of parenthood and overwhelmed by the patriarchy of it all. She found a low-level dealer, and then a mid-level supplier.

She masqueraded then as a black-market buyer, and was soon in contact with a man named Cervantes who claimed he bought directly from the *Sunrise Milk* factory, from a man named Siegfried.

Though he was a pig for profiting from the corruption of children, Alexandra befriended and then seduced Cervantes. She planted a surveillance chip in the heel of his left loafer while he slept.

The next day she tracked him to a nondescript three-story office building on the edge of the city. He entered through the public lobby and spoke briefly to a receptionist behind a counter. Then he disappeared through an interior door. Alex followed him in, motioning as if she were following him. The receptionist shrugged.

Behind the door was a manufacturing facility. Unlike the factories the *lecheros* dismantled, this one was high-tech, spacious, and clean. Workers in white coats and hard hats stood alongside belts where packets of powder and canisters of creamy liquid were churned and packaged and boxed. She glimpsed the logo on one of the crates: *Sunrise Milk*.

She looked about, noting an office perched on a suspended walkway that encircled the factory floor. But Cervantes had taken note that she'd followed him in.

"Gloria?" he said. She'd taken a pseudonym for her

undercover work. "What are you doing here?"

She hastily explained that she was cutting him out of her operation and coming directly to Siegfried for her supply of formula. Cervantes seemed unconcerned — she had not really done much work for him, anyway — and she hurried out, back to the community center.

"I have news for Mama Leche," she told the other lieutenants. "The location of a new formula factory. How do I contact her directly?"

They were jealous of her success, she knew, but they dutifully directed her to a small monitor at a wooden desk situated in the janitor's closet of the center. The monitor flickered green and black when she powered it on. She keyed in a short passcode and waited.

Soon the wavering visage of Mama Leche appeared. Alex related her story breathlessly, sparing no detail.

"Well done," Mama Leche said in her distorted alto voice. "Return to the factory. By yourself. Confront Siegfried. Warn him to cease operations or we will for him. Succeed and you will be given command of your own platoon."

Alex did as she was told. She returned to the factory as soon as she could that evening, only to find it empty. The receptionist was gone, and the clean equipment carted away. Siegfried had been warned! She thought back. Cervantes. He had spotted her and no doubt sounded the alarm. She imagined Mama Leche's disappointment in Alex's failure.

Then she spotted the office perched above. Her heart leapt. Perhaps there was some intelligence yet to be gleaned from something left behind.

The factory floor was covered with a thin layer of the formula dust. Alex padded across it, climbed the metal staircase to the walkway, and peeked into the office. She first saw the console: a cluster of buttons and dials, all surrounding a pair of speakers and what looked like a soundboard.

Then Alex knew: Siegfried had been intercepting Mama Leche's transmissions! That was how he always stayed ahead of the *lecheros*.

There was a rustle to her left, and she turned quickly to see the silhouette of a figure seated on a small stool in the dim corner of the office. Backlit from a small table-side lamp.

"Hello, *lechera*." A man's voice.

"Siegfried?"

"The very one. You're just a moment late."

"You can't outrun us forever," she said. She summoned up all of her confidence in Mama Leche and the *lecheros*. "We have nature on our side."

"We?" repeated Siegfried. His tone was self-assured in a way Alex's bravado couldn't be. "What do you think that is?" He motioned across the room to the console and the surveillance equipment.

"Receivers to intercept Mama Leche's transmissions, so you know when to run and hide."

"No, *lechera*, they're not receivers," said Siegfried. "They're transmitters."

Now, for the first time, Alex noticed what she hadn't before: a microphone and a script on the console. A small printer on a side table. A stack of the very pamphlets she had read that day on campus long ago. She shook her head.

"Now do you know who I am?" asked Siegfried. She hesitated for a long moment, shook her head again.

Finally she nodded, her voice quavered: "You're Mama Leche. But how?"

"Don't concern yourself with *how*," Siegfried said, "but rather *why*."

"Because you're wicked," Alex said.

"Hardly. I'm just a man seeking a profit."

"I'll tell the other *lecheros*."

"I regret that Mama Leche has already reported your betrayal to the others. You will not be welcome back."

Alex took her beret from her head and held it to her chest, dizzy from the revelation that her prophet was, in fact, the devil himself.

"You may as well keep that," Siegfried said, "as a token of a lesson learned."

Richard Walsh is the co-creator of The Adventures of Seamus Tripp, *a comedic adventure series that takes readers to a Victorian world of monsters, treasure, magic, and mystery. He works as an accountant and lives with his family and a pack of basset hounds in the suburbs of Minneapolis. Richard's short fiction has previously been featured in* Ama-Gi, Bewildering Stories, Bards & Sages Quarterly, *and several anthologies. Connect with him on Twitter at @rbwalsh_scifi. Find his works at* seamustripp.com.

Conformity is Mandatory
by Jonathan David Baird

The phone rang. I knew it was the interviewer. I had dreaded the call for the past hour. In the age of the internet no one wants to have actual face time with someone they may have to turn down for a job. So much easier to talk to them over the phone and make a decision based on that...and Facebook. No one makes a decision based on a resume any longer. It is all Facebook. If you lock down your profile, they think you are hiding something. Being too open about your life, they think you are not serious enough to hire. Facebook screws you coming and going...but no Facebook is worst of all. If you have no Facebook and you might as well not even apply. No one wants to hire an enigma in the age of the Internet. You can have everything an employer wants, but you must also have a life they can pick apart online.

I answer the phone.

"Hello."

The interviewer jumps right in. "Hi, Phillip this is Marcie from human resources at Stegal and Glass. We wanted to touch base after reading your resume and as you know we don't do formal interviews. We just like to chat a bit here on the phone and ask a few questions."

"Great," I answer, "I am an open book, ask me anything." **Here it comes**.

"Phillip do you go by your given name or is there another name you prefer to use?"

Yeah, fishing for some other name I might use on my Facebook profile. They can't come right out and say they want to check me out, but that is exactly what she is trying to do on the other side of this phone call.

"No Marcie, just Phillip. I am a pretty simple guy." You could hear the wheels turning in her head. She was silent for a moment.

"Well Phillip there is a quick question we ask all applicants."

I bet… all applicants she can't look up, I thought.

"Do you know who Sigmon and the Sea-monster are?"

What the F@#k?

"Excuse me Marcie? Sigmon and the who?"

"Sea-monster, it is just a question we like to break the ice with Phillip, sort of just open up a dialog with you. If you don't know that is fine."

This had taken a strange turn…was this actually the interviewer? Did I get a crank call who just went with the flow of the conversation?

"Marcie, I am at a loss to answer and I don't know what to say or who that is?" I hung up. I need the job. I got to have a job, but that was beyond strange. I think I will just make a Facebook profile and get it over with.

Jonathan David Baird has worked as an archaeologist for the past fifteen years throughout the Southeast. He left full-time field work in 2011 to finish graduate school. In 2012 Jonathan received a masters degree in English literature from Fort Hays State University. His focus of study was late Victorian Gothic horror. In 2014 he finished a second masters in American history with a focus on the frontier. Find his works at nukemars.com.

Doubleplusunhate
by George Donnelly

"I love you, Dad."

Marshal turned from his portscreen and looked at the boy. *Unspeak.* The rigid seat back pushed the thin slice of metal into his buttock. He pulled himself up from a slouch and looked back to his portscreen.

The boy climbed onto Marshal's lap. He knocked the portscreen from Marshal's hands and it clattered to the bare cement floor. Anger rose within him. "Doubleplusungood!"

The boy stared up at Marshal. His smile was wide and mischievous. Marshal studied his face. The deep blue eyes, the round face, the wide smile— Liker. Like... me.

Marshal jerked his head back as the realization struck him. "Doubleplusunhate. Doubleplusunhate Jak." He grabbed the boy and hugged him tight. Jak wrapped his thin sticks of arms around his father's neck. A jumble of emotions stirred in Marshal's gut but one word percolated to the top: defense.

***

"Jak forgetted goodpharm morewise. Ungood!" The woman smacked the back of her hand across Jak's face. Behind them was a gray wall. A small window provided limited access to the steel city. The buildings followed one another in silence, none reaching higher than the other.

Jake's face turned red. He tilted his head to one side and swallowed. He looked at Marshal. Marshal sat against the wall at the tiny kitchen table. He faced the window but kept his eyes to his portscreen.

"Hate!" yelled Jak. "Hate! Doubleplushate! Goodpharm ungood. Kill me, inner me. No! No morewise." He turned to his father. "Dad. Tell her."

His mother grabbed the boy by the shoulders and twisted him until he stood with his back to her. She pushed him towards the door. "Learnplace unlater, Jak! Go!"

"Dad," said Jak. His face fell and the beginnings of a frown formed around his mouth and eyes.

His mother glanced at Marshal. Her eyes were red and swollen. Her hands shook. She cleared her throat, grabbed Jak's bag from the floor and jammed it into his chest. She pushed him and he fell to the ground.

"Dad, please." Jak looked up at him from the floor. Water welled up and over his eyelids.

Marshal sighed. He put down the portscreen. The memory flashed in his mind. Jak's eyes. Unhateful. Knowwantingful. Unfrowning. Goodpharm ungave it. Goodpharm unlived Jak's … Marshal searched for the word. He imagined a ball of swirling, cereal-colored light inside of Jak. Soul. The Oldspeak came to him. His eyes darted from side to side and his forehead broke out in a sweat.

"Hate uncontrolled Jak! Hate Oldspeak!" yelled Jak's mother. She looked at Marshal. Her face was taut. She raised her chin and sneered. "Marshal crimethink." She nodded to herself. "Marshal unperson. Ownlife ungood. Oldspeak forbidded." She arched an eyebrow and took a step towards the door.

Time stopped for Marshal. He planned this day. He didn't want it but he expected it. He loved Johness. She once had Jak's same smile. But he loved Jak more. *Why did I have to teach Jak Oldspeak?* The feeling of the archaic language in his mind shocked him but he knew the answer.

"Joycamp fixwill Jak," said Johness. "Fixwill." She laid her hand on the doorknob.

Marshal stood up and threw his portscreen at the wall next to Johness. He was behind her. Marshal pulled the hunk of pointed metal from his back pocket and pushed it into the side of her neck. He stepped away from her and she fell backwards to the floor. Crimson liquid pooled on the gray floor next to her wriggling body.

Marshal thought back five years ago to when he first encountered the Oldpseak book in the domicile of a prole unperson. "Dictionary," it said in silver letters against a navy blue cover. The sharp, dry pages of forgotten words stirred an unexpected need in him. He steeled his resolve. *Doubleplushate crimethink ungood.* Ownlife. An ugly word. He translated it into Oldspeak. My own life. Jak's own life. He took in a rapid breath as the image of a tree sparked in his mind.

"We go." He pulled the boy up from the floor.

Jak's chest convulsed. "Mom," he whispered. Her body was

still. He leaned down and caressed her cheek. "I love you."

A man scowled at them in the doorway. Jak startled and the man saw Johness's body. His eyes went big and he took a step back.

Marshal kneeled down next to his wife's dead body. He extracted the makeshift knife. He ran to the door and forced the shiny metal deep into the man's chest. The man fell back into the corner and stared at the floor. Marshal reached for Jak's hand.

Jak took a step back. His mouth hung open and he shook his head.

Marshal grabbed Jak's upper arm and looked him in the eye. "Freedom, Jak. Freedom! Forest. New life. Unforget!"

***

"Slowful walk. Unfacecrime. Inair." Marshal smoothed out the wrinkles in Jak's shirt and pushed his hair to one side. "Untense." The sidewalk was crowded.

Jak nodded and let his breath out fast. His pace accelerated.

"Slowful." Marshal scrunched up his face then let the muscles fall. *Freedom.* He stared straight ahead and made for the movestop in lockstep with Jak.

At the movestop, a group gathered. People and transports streamed in all directions. Crowds gathered for the quick morning ration in a sprawling square cornerwise from him. Big Brother's cartoonish visage streamed from building to building in a digital display of omnipresence. People dressed in white, silver, tan and sky blue laid eyes on him. *Facecrime!* He raged at himself for his lapse.

The white transport eased to a stop in front of them. The doors slid open. Marshal redoubled his grip on Jak's small hand. His heart leapt with joy and he struggled to contain his ungood emotion.

"Killer!" The ragged voice came from behind him. "Unproceed killer Marshal."

Marshal froze. Jak's grip tightened and trembled. Marshal sneered at his own incompetence.

"Killer unproceed. Thinkpol come," said the neighbor. The giant screens on the buildings changed. Big Brother's face appeared larger now. His eyes raged and a giant finger pointed down at Marshal.

The crowd formed into lines and moved away from the pair. The square fell silent. Passengers filed out of the back door of the transport. The front doors closed mere centimeters from Marshal's nose.

"Dad. I love you."

Marshal didn't want to look down at his boy but he steeled himself. His heart crushed. Gravity pulled hard at the boy's eyes and mouth. *I doed crimethink. I doed ... did this.* He imagined the boy in joycamp.

No. The thought catalyzed a chain reaction of decision within him. Marshal whipped around and shook a finger at his accuser. "Oldthinker!" he yelled. He narrowed his eyes and strode towards the older man. "Blackwhite ungoodpharm oldthinker bewill unperson!"

The man staggered back, his eyes wide. "No," he whispered. "Doubleplusgood duckspeaker. Ingsoc bellyfeel."

Marshal turned and ran down the block. They turned left, ran down another block and the crowds were there again. They boarded a transport and stared straight ahead. Marshal rubbed his thumb into the palm of Jak's hand. *Bewill good. Bewill good.*

George Donnelly is the author of space opera, robot apocalypse and dystopian science fiction series. A rebel and unreformed idealist, he believes equally in human rights and abundant hugs before bedtime. Get a new free short story every month at georgedonnelly.com.

Paradoxes of Water Filtration
by Jon Garett and Richard Walsh

It was going to be another cloudless day onboard the Freestead *Mayflower*. The sun was peeking over the eastern horizon, and a cool breeze blew off the ocean. Tendrils of mist still clung to the surface of the water, but they'd burn off in minutes. The central engines hummed. The omnipresent mega-shoals of fish trailed slowly behind in their aquaculture enclosures. The omnipresent mega-flocks of seabirds trailed slowly behind them, not yet harnessed successfully into an aeroculture venture.

Angus Journeyman arrived at his office three minutes after sunrise. The inside temp was pleasant, maintained efficiently by a state-of-the-art regulator and continual adjustment algorithm. But that was as much as he understood about heating and cooling. The seastead included environs as varied as the high-density residences in the heart of the ship and the single-family luxury units floating high overhead, so several specialized firms ran those functions on the 'stead. He employed a small upstart called *Envirolution HVAC* to maintain optimal comfort and efficiency in his office.

Angus seated himself and proceeded through his morning routine, built on the ORDER productivity method:

Organize, Roster, Dashboard, Efficiency, Reprioritize

First on the list: Organize. Angus reviewed his calendar. His day was full of sales calls, team meetings, and a Q&A session with his "Positive Flow" clients, those customers whose rainwater collection equipment added to the net volume of the system. They tended to be his stingiest, most demanding clients, but critical ones as well: innovative, cost-conscious, and an essential supply of new water.

Second: Roster. Full complement of office staff, with an unusual amount of activity already in the outer office. A stack of vid chat windows were open on each of the four monitors. Even his shy bookkeeper, Marion, was typing on one session while speaking into her Lyncset for another.

Only the engineer, George Dunmuch, was absent, though his badge scan showed that he had arrived at the water works before anyone else. Dunmuch was the sole staff holdover from the acquisition, and he was a mechanical genius, if unorthodox in his methods. No doubt he would show up soon, covered in grease or some smoldering sealant.

Third: Dashboard. Angus toggled over to the firm's operations summary and reviewed the previous day's performance. In short: not good. Two more lost clients and a sharp increase in incoming calls to the firm's overwhelmed administrative office. That explained the bustle outside his door. If they were unable to get the condensers back to 80% capacity, there'd be hell to pay: more complaints and more clients lost to their rivals, *Tres Aguas* and *RainWay*.

Water reclamation was a critical service for the Freestead, which was why the floating city's inhabitants trusted it to three profit-seeking competitors rather than one centrally-planned monopoly. The clients who had left *Scudy Springs* yesterday were already transitioning to their new providers this morning, and they would likely never switch back.

Angus had bought the firm from old Scudy Molino six months earlier. It'd been at a discount, and now Angus knew the full extent why. Molino had been honest at the time of the sale: the company's old equipment needed to be replaced, not repaired, to keep up with *Tres Aguas* and *RainWay*. Those firms had already implemented the Vapoplasma tech that was commonplace on the larger seasteads.

"Change management" was a phrase Angus loved. It conjured up concepts like synergies and dovetailing and Gantt charts. But he had underestimated just how much change he'd need to manage as owner of *Scudy Springs*.

Old Scudy had taken the cash from the sale to retire up in one of the Photic-Tower Spheres that floated hundreds of meters above the seastead, tethered there like full-service, self-sustaining luxury dirigibles. Angus was left behind to get condenser capacity back to 80%. He wondered what the sunrises looked like from the Towers.

Fourth: <u>E</u>fficiency. Capacity was projected to fall again. Probably to 77.8%. Outside chance all the way to 77.5%. The corresponding drop in clients was inevitable.

Angus pinged Dunmuch, unable to wait for him to

materialize in the office.

"Likely the micro-screen filters," said the old engineer via the cyberchat. By the sounds of it, he was in the one of the engineering substations beneath the seastead's main platform. "When they reach saturation condenser efficiency falls off quick."

"Can you clean them?"

"Nope. Once saturated they gotta be replaced."

New filters. Angus switched lines over to a chat with Jordana, the firm's general manager.

"We're going to need to buy replacement parts," he said. "Micro-screen filters to fit our AR2030 condensers. Where's the nearest 'stead?"

A slight pause while she pulled the geodata. "300 kilometers southwest," she said. "The *Mises Garden*. Course is southwest. Away from us. Navi-Planner estimates round trip is 27.2 hours. Assuming you can get one of the faster high-speed transports."

"Unlikely, and too long, anyway. Anyone north of us that'll bring them closer?"

"Nope. *Mises* is the only 'stead within 500 clicks."

"Other options?"

"There's one, though I don't think you'll like it." She messaged him a map of their position. "We're only about 20 kilometers off PacWest."

North America. PacWest was the state administering the upper northwest of the continent. Their course, south-by-southwest on the Pacific's northern current, was taking them along the west coast of the North American Union.

Fifth: <u>R</u>eprioritize. "It'll have to do. Set up a hover-barge. I'll get a merc company. We leave in an hour."

At least he had an excuse to postpone the Positive Flow Q&A another day.

***

Twenty clicks by hover-barge was a lot choppier than by seastead. They were closer to the water, for one thing, and the waves intensified as they approached land.

But they moved fast, and the seven Aesir Security mercs he'd hired to accompany them were accustomed to this type of thing. All seven were military veterans of one stripe or another: former NAU grunts who'd fought the endless brush fires that had popped up during trans-continental unification or South American mercenaries out of work since the Pan-American governments had succumbed to international pressures and shut down their militias.

The mercs were well-trained, well-armed, and - Angus ruminated — well-paid.

Dunmuch, the ninth passenger on the hover-barge, was also unfazed by the motion over the choppy waves. Twenty years asea, even on an island city, would inure you to that sort of thing.

They transited the Columbia River without issue, but the arrival of a Freestead boat elicited an inhospitable reaction from the government-owned Portland Urban District Dock Authority (PUDDA). His small party was required to mill about the stuffy, dilapidated PUDDA office for 45 minutes while Angus filled out paperwork to clear their trip. Literal *paper*work. A bureaucratic holdover from fifty years before. Long since extinct on the seasteads, replaced by electronic documentation because of paper's weight, inefficiency, and propensity to be lost just when it was needed.

The Aesir team had brought their own ground transport aboard the hover-barge: an eight-wheel, 15-person "Caterpillar," which was a blown-up version of the sci-fi lander from *Moon Patrol,* the antique arcade game Angus had played as a kid. It featured a big, open cockpit, a gun turret on top (if the situation came to that), and ample cargo space in the belly.

Once they cleared PUDDA customs, they set off for the heart of the district, where Angus had set up a noon meeting with a mid-level government rep who was selling the filter replacements. It was half-past noon already.

Angus and Dunmuch sat in the cockpit next to Colonel Fortis, their Aesir Security senior agent. Fortis was a tiny Quechuan with dark, unblinking eyes. Her name had been a byword in biotech security and recovery before she had emigrated to the first of the Freesteads. It was now whispered that, despite her field activity, she owned a controlling share of Aesir.

"Good thing we got these overfilled tires," Fortis said, referencing the deplorable state of the State roads. They hardly noticed the bumps and jostling, with the off-road suspension, but the huge ruts and piles of rubble meant the road would be nearly impassable for smaller vehicles.

"That's probably the point," Angus said. "Populace has to stay put in the Urban District when the roads are this bad."

"And we're heading into the heart of it," said Dunmuch. "The heart of the beast."

"Indeed. 'PORTLAND: WHERE HAPPINESS IS A BASIC HUMAN RIGHT,'" Angus said, reading a billboard standing alongside the road.

"When everyone's happy, no one's happy," said Fortis.

Five kilometers and 40 minutes later they arrived at an unmarked warehouse in an industrial zone. Wire fencing surrounded a grim concrete yard. Security cameras, probably unpowered and unmonitored, bristled atop high poles.

Angus, Fortis, and Dunmuch climbed down out of the Caterpillar. Fortis ordered the six other mercs to stand watch from within. Angus didn't pay much attention to the command, preoccupied as he was with the upcoming transaction.

They were greeted by a squat, mustachioed man bundled against the autumn weather by a heavy coat. This was Donny "Skog" Skoglund, Angus's government contact. Four tall, plains-clothed men slouched behind him, making no effort to conceal their underarm holsters.

"I've got those filters," said Skog. "Top of the line. Bleeding-edge. Half our processors can't even deploy these yet. Bleeding-freakin'-edge."

He motioned through a doorway, into the dark interior of the warehouse. Fortis gave a barely perceptible shake of her head.

"Bring them out here," said Angus evenly. The peril of the setting struck him for the first time. The desperation in the bureaucrat's voice. The open display of force. "If the equipment's as good as you say we'll buy them all. May as well inspect them in the open."

Skog arched an eyebrow but ordered two of his toughs to carry out the crates. It required four trips total, but he did not order the other pair to assist.

They finally opened the crates, and Dunmuch stepped forward to inspect each, pulling the large filters from the containers, checking the manufacturer's seal, and cross-checking serial codes against an inventory app.

"They check out," he said after fifteen minutes of meticulous inspection.

"What did I tell you?" said Skog. "Top of the line. Bleeding-edge."

"We'll take your word for it," said Dunmuch.

"Ha. You're the businessman," Skog said to Angus with a wink. "Water's precious. Therefore you can say anything to justify your prices. Now that you've got a crate of new filters, acquired through your hard work, you can jack up rates on your customers!"

"You have no idea," Angus said, not bothering to correct the poor man's misconception. Life in the State-dominated bureaucracy of Portland had completely distorted his notion of how prices worked in a free market.

"So how can I pay you?" Angus continued. "Seastead credits? Or NAU ameros?"

"Credits, credits," said Skog. "They'll be worth the same

the next time you cycle through. Ameros?" He shrugged. "Who knows."

Angus passed over a cred card with the balance loaded, and Skog ordered his men to load the crates into the back of the Caterpillar. Their eyes widened to see the half-dozen mercs waiting within.

"Nothing to be scared of," said Fortis. "They're for just in case." And she winked, too.

The trip out was as bumpy and slow as the trip in. Angus smiled to see the back of the billboard they'd passed earlier, where someone had spraypainted a response.

PORTLAND: THE EQUAL DISTRIBUTION OF MISERY, it read.

His smile faded quickly, however. They slowed around a bend in the road and came upon a makeshift checkpoint, obviously thrown up in the two hours since they'd passed earlier. A small, quasi-official sign stuck into the ground read "Citizens' Safety Check." A trio of heavily-armed soldiers had erected a barrier of miscellaneous construction debris and were waving for the truck to pull over and stop.

Angus instantly, unconsciously, transitioned to crisis-management mode. Risks, operational planning, next steps, contingencies. And in the next instant he realized that he hadn't considered any situation like this. That he had no idea what to do.

He turned to Fortis, to tell her to slow down and he'd try to talk to them. Probably pay a hefty bribe. Hopefully that was all these soldiers were after. The costs of this trip were rising by the minute.

But Fortis wasn't waiting for his orders. She was the security expert, not him. He had hired Aesir so he *wouldn't* have to think of what to do in this situation, and it was a good thing, too, because Fortis had no intention of stopping. She slowed the truck enough to give two of her mercs time to man the overhead turret, and then she hit the gas, accelerating the huge Caterpillar straight toward the flimsy wall of barrels and wood scraps. The engine roared. The mercs above opened fire on the barricade, though the small squad of government soldiers had already begun to disperse at the first sign of resistance. The truck smashed through the barrier with barely a pause.

"Well done," said Angus when they were a kilometer clear. His heart was still racing.

"A pretty minor incident," said Fortis. "The firm would hate to make a liability payment to *Scudy Springs* for a minor incident."

***

The next day's <u>ORDER</u> showed significant improvements across the board.

The condensers were up to 84.3% efficiency, even with the outdated filters Skog had sold them.

On the trip home, Dunmuch had mentioned an idea for improving *Scudy*'s reclamation tech: a nanomesh strain that could be installed at critical junctions, reducing utilization of the micro-screens. As they'd discussed it, he'd had an idea for how the nanomesh could be also used to clean and recycle existing filters. The material was already in use on Freestead *Nebuchadnezzar*, a much better supply chain than having to rely on returning to the continent for replacement parts.

Jordana reported that client complaints had already decreased. Angus would never be able to raise rates, despite the efforts of the day before, but their mission had at least stopped the exodus of unhappy customers. *Scudy Springs* remained competitive for another day.

Under Organize: he groaned to himself. The Positive Flow Q&A was scheduled for 0930 that morning.

Jon Garett & Richard Walsh live and write in Minneapolis, Minnesota. They have previously published in the anthologies Perchance to Dream *and* The Great Tome of Forgotten Relics and Artifacts. *They are the creators of* The Adventures of Seamus Tripp, *a comic adventure series that combines monsters, treasure, magic, and mystery. The series can be found at seamustripp.com. Connect with them on Twitter at @jongarett and at @rbwalsh_scifi.*

Ghost Writer
by Vaughn Treude

It was a typical day in the unemployment office, the usual parade of victims of the recession. Some were slackers gaming the system; others were desperate. Typical, that is, until he arrived.

He was an older fellow, mid-fifties. Too young to retire, but older than companies wanted to hire. These days, there were a lot of folks in that position.

"Not receiving your checks, huh? Let's see what we can do about that." The caseworker brought up the man's file on the computer and skimmed it. "I see you've been without a job for some time. I don't understand why a man with your credentials is still unemployed."

The client smiled. There was a weariness in his eyes that went beyond the bags and crow's feet. "It's an interesting story," he began.

***

I was once an up and coming sci-fi writer. My novel *Whither the Stars of Orion* was nominated for the Nebula award. The next two sold well, but not as well as the publisher had hoped, so they dropped me.

Royalties dropped off, my wife got laid off, and money was really tight. Then one day on the Internet, I encountered a mysterious ad.

Sci-Fi Script Writers Wanted for TV pilots. Salary, benefits, private office.

I called the number. Bob, the Company's in-house recruiter, was a real friendly guy. He knew my work, asked about my family, and raved about what a great opportunity this was. We talked money and benefits but the work itself was vague.

"We're doing a stealth campaign to promote an upcoming project. You know the entertainment industry; can't let the competition know what we're doing."

"Will I be allowed to work from home?"

"Sorry, but no. And there's a non-disclosure clause, of course."

He emailed me the contract and I skimmed it quickly. "I don't have a problem with the Company retaining the rights, but I don't want to be a ghost writer. When the movie or whatever comes out, I want credit for my work, to help me restart my career. And I'd love to be on the creative team that writes the script. Can I get a clause in the contract to that effect?"

"No problem. I'll have Ira write something up and send it back to you ASAP."

Despite my reservations, it was too good to pass up. The Company was located in an office park near the airport. It was a nondescript place, with cubicles full of employees working quietly at their computers. They gave me a private office with a window.

Eddie, my new boss, did my orientation. "I haven't read your novels, but the reviews are impressive. They rave about your attention to scientific detail."

"Thanks. So what's this project about?"

"Are you familiar with The *X-Files*?"

"Huge fan."

"Then it's your lucky day." He explained that I'd be spinning conspiracy theories about real-world events. "We'll start out with short pieces, teasers for the project. If the first release makes money we have several sequels planned."

"Theories about what?"

"Oh, the JFK assassination, the Boston Marathon bombing, and 9/11 for starters."

"Really? I don't think I'd be comfortable with exploiting other peoples' tragedies."

"You seen *Sophie's Choice*? *Schindler's List*? If they can write stories about the Holocaust, why not 9/11?"

"Really? Like *Schindler's List*?" I thought, could this be Spielberg's secret new project?

Eddie shrugged and gave me a knowing smile.

My assignments were hardly Spielberg material. Take 9/11 for example. You've heard the 'inside job' theories, right? Some of them are possible, I suppose. But the stories they assigned me were crazy, Enquirer stuff, written like factual news reports.

For example, the planes that hit the towers weren't real,

they were holograms. The government landed the real planes at a field on Long Island, and took the passengers to a detention center somewhere. Or the planes were real, and there were these mysterious pods under the wings. I'm particularly proud of that one, because I photo-shopped the images to accompany the story.

How about this one: When the towers collapsed, the first responders found a lake of molten gold. My absolute favorite is how all the hijackers' names can be found in the Cairo phone book, so they must all be alive. Not many guys in Egypt named Mohammad, are there?

This stuff went on for years. At first it was fun, but after a while I became impatient. What would happen when this gig was over? The pay and benefits were great, but my family kept pressing me for details that I couldn't give them. How the hell was this supposed to restart my career?

Then one day I saw one my stories on the Internet, on one of the 'alt news' sites, presented as fact. At first I laughed out loud. I wanted to show it to my wife, but the contract was so strict, I was hesitant to do that. So I went to Eddie.

"You saw that, huh?" he laughed. "Good! All part of the marketing plan, create buzz."

"Does that mean there's no more gag order?"

"No! You must tell no one unless we say otherwise. Trust me, it's for the best."

As time went on, I saw more of these stories. A bunch of them got compiled into a You-tube video called *Spare Change* or something like that. But there was no sign of a movie deal.

Eddie refused to address my concerns. "You're getting paid, aren't you? Like I said, be patient. It'll all work out in the end."

"But it's been years. Bob promised me I'd get credit for it, and I'd get to work on the movie. If that never happens, that's breach of contract."

Eddie stared at me. "I'm aware of no such clause."

"I have a copy of the email from him on my computer."

"OK, let's pull up your contract." He tapped a few keys, then turned the monitor around to show me. "Sorry, there's nothing like that in here."

"Well, ask Bob. He promised to send me an updated contract."

"You mean Bob Peterson? Sorry, he's no longer associated with the company."

"This is bullshit! What if I quit?"

"Then according to the contract, you'll have to forfeit 100% of your advance."

"What? That's outrageous! You can't hold me to this contract! It's invalid! I'll sue!"

Eddie sighed. "Are you sure you want to quit? We're really happy with your work."

"Yes, I'm sure. I want out of here."

"Fine. Sign this release and you may resign with no fiscal penalties but no severance. Ira will have your wages to date for you at the front desk."

When I went home to tell my wife, she said, "What the hell did you do that for?"

"They were exploiting me. I'm standing up for my rights!"

"Really?" She picked up a stack of bills from the table and waved them in my face. "How about standing up for these?"

"It'll be okay. Now I can write for myself again."

I had big ideas for promoting my books and writing new ones. I called my agent and to run them by him. Before I could say anything, he said, "Where have you been? While you were busy being invisible, your books have all been removed from publication."

"What? Even *Stars*? Stan, call Galactic Publishing and chew them out!"

"What good will that do? Galactic said they sold all the rights to a third party."

"Oh yeah? You asshole! Is this what I'm paying you for?"

"What pay? You're lucky I took your call, jerk." He hung up, and that was the last I heard from him.

No problem; self-publishing was taking off, and I had lots of ideas. Before joining the Company I'd had a book mostly finished. I took me only a few weeks to finish it, then I posted it on Amazon.

Three days later I got a notice from them. My new e-book, *Stars Revisited*, had been removed from the site due to a claim of copyright infringement by some gal I've never heard of in Pennsylvania.

We went round and round with the phone calls and the attorneys, and while they hashed it out, I wrote a couple stories and a novella, and posted them on Barnes and Noble. You guessed it, same thing. Each one supposedly infringing on a different writer, all assorted nobodies.

By this time, I'd gotten the hint. Those bastards at the Company were trying to ruin what little was left of my career. My wife was breathing down my neck, so I figured I had to get a regular job.

I have a degree in computer science, and before I got published, I spent a few years working as a programmer. I updated my resume and put it on all the sites. There were calls from recruiters, but every time I'd be close to getting the job, something would come up to prevent it. One place said my SSN belonged to a 90-year old black woman. Then I was on the terrorist watch list. Next I supposedly owed $50,000 in back taxes. After that, I was on the sex offender registry. It was always something different, and by the time I'd clear up the error, the job would have gone to somebody else.

I finally got a job as a barista for a coffee shop by the college and worked there for six months, when one of my fellow employees realized he had one of my books. He showed it to my employer, who asked me to sign his copy. A few days later I was terminated. They never gave me any reason.

In the meantime, with no income, I lost my house, my wife left me, and the bank repossessed my car. I live in a converted bus behind my ex-brother-in-law's house, and I came here on a bicycle. You may not believe me, but it's all the God's honest truth.

***

"Holy moly," the caseworker said, "That's one of the most unusual stories I've ever heard. But don't worry, I'm sure we can find you something. In the meantime, let's take care of that problem with your unemployment checks."

"I'd appreciate that."

"Just give me your social, and I'll bring up your file. Oh, I see your problem."

He sighed. "What is it this time? My number doesn't match? I'm an illegal alien? My mother's in the Taliban?"

"You owe back child support. The money's being sent to Layla Taylor in Lubbock, Texas."

"Child support? I don't have any kids! I've never even been to Lubbock!"

"Well, if it's an error, I'm sure we can get it cleared up. But I was thinking about what you said. My neighbor's brother's housekeeper went to this seminar on 9/11 and she told me about those pods. Said they had ironclad proof of those things under the wings."

"I told you, I photo-shopped it! That's my picture!"

"And the thing about the hijackers being alive, that's definitely true. I read that myself on *The Shizer Report*."

The client got all red in the face and began to shout. "No no, no! I made that up!"

"Keep it down, sir!" The caseworker snapped. "Here, I'll get you the address of the court in Lubbock." As he waited for the computer to respond, he shook his head and smiled. "I just knew it was all an inside job. Just wait until my girlfriend hears about this!"

"Were you even listening? I don't know who did it for what

reason. I don't know who killed Princess Di, or where Elvis is currently living. I can only tell you which conspiracy theories that I invented. And I invented a lot of them!"

"Wow," the caseworker said, as if letting it sink in. "I didn't believe him at the time, but I guess my cousin's auto mechanic's dentist really did see Saddam Hussein skiing in Aspen…"

Vaughn Treude grew up on a farm in North Dakota. The remoteness of his home, with few children his age nearby, made science fiction and fantasy a welcome escape. His favorite writers included Asimov, Heinlein, and Tolkien. He always planned to become a writer, but the demands of life kept his projects from completion. After several years in software, he realized that the same discipline required for engineering could be applied to creating fictional worlds. Find his works at vaughntreude.com.

Icky
by Frank Marcopolos

Enzo Prinziatta had passed out—the light-headedness, the dizziness, the nausea, the sweating, the bodily crumple onto the restaurant floor—after hearing that his evangelical father had actually voluntarily ceased living in order to go to Heaven and be with God, and did not die as a result of a shark-fishing accident as Enzo had been told for years. (This devastating news came, too, close on the heels of Enzo's decision to leave his pregnant ex-girlfriend to transfer to a bigger university, where his chances of being drafted would be better.) After he was revived, his friends and family all agreed that what he needed most was a "spa weekend." He initially laughed, then thought it ungodly, then wondered if Jesus had gotten massages. But the friends and the family kept insisting, kept raving about the local-famous massage parlor up at the Mohonk Mountain House Resort in New Paltz, known for its recuperative powers. And, of course, his mom and step-dad, Leonard, would just have to come along. For comfort. Or safety. Or something.

"Look at this picture," Leonard said, staring at a framed

painting on the wall of Enzo's hotel room when they first got there.

"I think it's a painting, actually," Enzo said.

"Whatever," Leonard said. "It's of whatshisname. From the Greeks. The Greek myths. If I can just remember."

Enzo, unpacking, glanced over. "Icarus? I think I read about him once. I forget what his deal was."

"Looks like... see how faded he looks?" Leonard said. "Almost like he doesn't exist. Especially, I mean, look at the other colors. They're all so bold, and stuff. And poor little Icky right here. Seems like he's fading away."

"Icky?" Enzo said. He liked to unpack carefully, finding a separate drawer, shelf, or hanger for each category of his clothing.

"Oh! That's right! Now I remember," Leonard said. "If you think about it, Icky's main problem was that he didn't listen to dear old dad. That's what it was."

"Gee. How surprising of you to say something like that," Enzo said. "Couldn't have predicted that in a million years." He hung two wrinkly, button-down shirts in the closet.

"Yeah, see, his dad was this great and grand craftsman, buddy, and he made these wings for the both of them to escape from this prison they were in. I don't know why they were in prison. But he warned little Icky. He warned him, he said, 'Hey! Don't fly too low because the humidity from the water will slow you down too much, but also don't fly too high because then the sun will melt the wax that holds the wings on.' See, he was giving good fatherly advice like that, Enzo."

"So, what did Icarus do?" Enzo said. He dropped his t-shirts in the top drawer of the dresser, his underwear in the middle, and socks on the bottom.

"Well, like any young man, Icky felt a little rebellion in his loins and he decided to ignore dear old dad and fly right close to the sun. Which led to this here," Leonard said. He pointed at the painting. "Plunksville. Right next to Deadtown."

"I don't think liars should be dispensing, like, wisdom or whatever," Enzo said. He laid a pair of jeans on the floor of the closet beneath the button-downs.

"Enzo, we didn't lie. Your mom and me, we were just trying to protect you, okay?" Leonard said, his eyebrows raised for emphasis. "Protecting you is a good thing. You're acting like it's a bad thing, Enzo. We were looking out for you."

"I get it, Leonard. You absolve yourself of all blame. Very convenient for you, but I get it," Enzo said. "Vaya con Dios."

"Just think about it, Enzo," Leonard said. "Your family loves you. We love you, Enzo."

"Lies are not love," Enzo said.

Leonard shook his head, with a look of defiance in his eyes, and left the room. He was scheduled to play tennis with Enzo's mom in ten minutes.

Enzo removed the last item from his baggage—a rosary— and hung it off the left corner of the frame of the Icarus painting. It swayed a few times before settling into place.

***

Walking down to his massage appointment, Enzo started thinking about Shannon and the baby in her belly and how all the troubles started and his high school Spanish teacher, Mr. Rodriguez, saying, "Never speel the seed!" Everything was so conflated. Enzo didn't want to spill the seed, but sometimes life made it hard to heed good advice.

In the calmly-colored massage room, he sat down on a cushiony table and waited for the large muscle-bound Swedish woman who would manipulate his muscles into a state of "harmonic bliss" as promised by the brochure he'd read. The Venetian blinds were drawn up on the one window in the room, and through it Enzo could see one of the resort's pools. The area looked abandoned, even though it was a bright, shiny afternoon. There was only one person in the pool. That one person was a little girl, about seven years old in a blue, old-fashioned, one-piece bathing suit and swimming cap. He wondered why her parents did not seem to be around. No one at all seemed to be watching her.

The masseuse came in. She wasn't Swedish, wasn't large, and wasn't mannish at all. She was young and blonde, with big, blue eyes framed by black, winged eyeliner. Her thin body was covered by a flowy white summer dress, and she was barefoot, with white-tipped toenails. "Hi," she said, as if this were the standard masseuse greeting worldwide, and she had said it thousands of times, but she always made the extra customer-service effort to make it seem warm and friendly, not some tradecraft formality. "I'm Cristy."

"Hello," Enzo said with his head down, trying to hide how nervous he felt. He wasn't exactly sure how God felt about seed-spilling during massages, even if Mr. Rodriguez from Sacred Cross certainly would not have approved. Enzo thought a large Swedish woman with man-hands might have been better.

"You can take off your robe, lie on your stomach, facing the window now," Cristy said, as if by rote, but again infused with customer-service friendliness.

"Can we, I'm a little nervous about this, actually," Enzo said. "My parents, they're all on my case about something, and I can't, I mean, I haven't had a lot of time to talk to someone who doesn't want me to do this or that? Would that be okay or no? If we just talked?"

Cristy said, "It's your time. For me, it's an hour either way. So, we can talk and if there's time left, we can still do the massage, if you want."

"That seems organized," Enzo said. He looked through the window, and saw the little girl in the pool, swimming a Trudgen stroke. He thought that *someone* should be supervising the kid. Maybe someone in fact was, he thought, but he just couldn't see them. "Did you ever feel kind of like that all of the people in your life, your family and all of your friends, are all wanting to, I don't know, were like, hiding stuff from you? Like your parents and stuff?" Enzo said.

"Honey, I'm from Poughkeepsie," Cristy said. "I'm just happy they were around." She chuckled. "They're not exactly Parents of the Year. But they're cool, though."

"I always thought if I had something, some talent or skill, to get me out of Brooklyn, it would be a good thing. But it seems like it's turning into kind of a nightmare," Enzo said. "I don't even know if I'm making sense. I've kind of been going through a rough time lately."

"I'm so sorry, sweetie. So what's this big skill you got?" Cristy said. "I'm curious now."

"God hath granted me the power of a super-fast fastball," Enzo said.

"Ah," she said. "Baseball. Good deal."

"You would think, yeah."

"Well, you know what they say about diamonds and pressure and all that," Cristy said.

"Yeah. The Bible says, Blessed is the man who remains steadfast under trial," Enzo said. "I guess."

"So, this fastball of yours," Cristy said. "Are we talking major leagues, or like, just a nice college thing?"

Enzo said, "It's, like, got the potential to go pro, yeah."

"Really?" she said, surprise in her voice. The expression in her wing-framed eyes subtly changed from that of casual, professional indifference to enamored attraction. "You know what? You should let me give you a deep-tissue PoughTown-special massage. Relax your mind and body. It'll be the best. Experience. Of your life, I promise." Her tone was dripping with double-entendric meaning. "Just relax, and I'll begin rubbing some essential oils in. Some people feel more comfy with their undies on, some feel more comfy with 'em off. It's totally up to you, either way, so there's no pressure. It's whatever. But off is a more total and relaxing experience, and I totes recommend it."

"I'm gonna go ahead and keep mine on, if that's okay," Enzo said. He saw, blurrily, the little girl in the water outside splashing around wildly, panic-crazed. It seemed, too, like she was screaming out for help. "Uhhh. There's a kid out there, seems to be in trouble."

"Oh," said Cristy, spilling some oil on her hands. "Can't be. That part of the resort's closed right now."

"Really?" Enzo said. He saw the child splashing around the pool in distress, however. As she was flapping around, she still seemed to be yelling. "I'm sorry. I gotta…" He hopped off the table and ran out.

Cristy yelled after him, panic in her voice, "Wait! Hey! Lemme finish you, ahh, I can make you feel… not icky!"

That last word caught his attention. "Weird," he thought, as he ran out of the building, frantically looking around for lifeguards, adults, anyone. Then he got to the pool. There was no girl, no splashing, no nothing. No evidence that something dramatic had just happened, that the girl had been saved, or that anyone had been out there anytime recently.

"What's happening to me?" Enzo said to no one. He yanked his cross pendant off its chain around his neck and threw them both, chain and cross, into the pool. He stripped off his underwear, then squatted down to pick up a jagged-edged pebble. He cut a cross into his left upper arm, then jumped into the pool and sank down to the bottom.

Enzo felt a buoyant kind of peace, a bubbly, chemical-laden overwhelm that felt calming, relaxing, serene. It was as if there were nothing that could be done, so there was nothing to do, like a good lazy Sunday after church. He heard a crash above his head. Before he could figure out what was happening, he felt a tug on his right arm toward the surface of the pool. A beleaguered kind of resignation washed over him. He went with it. As they got near the top, the other person released him and seemed to splash up onto the concrete lip of the pool.

Enzo felt disoriented as he tried to adjust to this surprise. He hopped, more or less and splashily, up on the concrete, then realized that he was in fact naked. He curled up, trying to cover his naturalness.

"Don't worry, sweetie," Cristy the masseuse said. "I've seen it all." Her winged eyeliner webbed downward in branching rivulets.

Even though she was soaking wet and beautiful in that 'caught in the rain' way he'd seen in movies so many times, Enzo felt no sexual desire for Cristy in that moment. In that moment, he simply felt his left upper arm burning and pulsating. Enzo heard footsteps coming toward the pool, and then Leonard's voice: "Hey, what the heck is going on here, Mister Icky?" Enzo looked up and watched Leonard take a bite of an ambrosia apple. "Don't call me that," he said.

"Oh?" said Leonard. "What *should* we call you, then? Ooh, this ain't ripe!" He basketball-shot the apple toward a nearby garbage can. It struck the rim of the can and rolled into the shade of a small, fake Mediterranean Cypress tree.

Frank Marcopolos is a former U.S. paratrooper (82nd Airborne Division) turned literary fiction author and voice-over artist. He currently lives in Austin, Texas with his pet tetra, Fredward. The story Icky *will appear, in slightly altered form, as a part of Frank's forthcoming novel, due to be published by Thanksgiving, 2016. Find his works at frankmarcopolos.com.*

Trial by Twit
by George Donnelly

"It's just not working out."

She glared at me from the other side of our spacious forty square meter capsule, her eyes red and puffy.

Something heavy fell loose in my chest and I walked to her. "Look, baby, it's not you, it's me. I'm—"

She pushed me away. The look said it all — hurt, hate, vulnerability, pain. "You're damned right it's you. I'm breaking up with you! Get out now. I want you back in Broseg in time for lunch!"

"Now wait. I broke up with you." This was veering dangerously off track.

Emmeline was a good girl. She cooked, cleaned and screwed on schedule. She just wasn't for me. There was no oomph, no chemistry, no excitement. She was just a boring mid-level executive at a fully automated cheese puff manufactory.

She had no greater aspirations. Didn't even want to travel. Only wanted one kid. Hated the forest. I mean, come on, zzzzzzzzz.

She pulled that sheet of paper from her bra drawer.

"So you've been planning this?"

"I'm on record at the MMA as having initiated this process the same day I pulled you out of Broseg." She gave me that raised eyebrow.

She thought she was so smart. I guess she was. I was cornered. The Men's Management Administration would consider it an open and shut case. Recidivist man disappoints woman. Man is remitted to Broseg. It was the most common story, hundreds of cases per week. There'd be no appeal. They wouldn't even listen to my objections.

"Not only," she said, her lips pursed as if dealing with a disagreeable insect, "are you losing your regular lay and your home, but you're broke. I'm filing for half of everything you have. And the other half of your pathetic savings will burn up in taxes and fees. You're back to zero, Nick. You'll be borrowing again in a week. Too bad you didn't think of that before you refused to wash the dishes."

The shake was coming on. That thing where my body vibrates and I can't control it. My voice goes up a few octaves and my throat seizes up. I go cold. Yeah, that was happening. I took three deep breaths but the shake frequency increased.

I'd spent fifteen months, three weeks, two days and twelve hours building up that nest egg. I'd scrubbed toilets, programmed robots, planted sorghum, harvested tilapia and extracted semen from gorillas.

Along the way, I got three skin infections, one acute case of hantavirus, a broken arm from a freaked out bot, random and assorted lacerations and a frisky hug from Coconut, the local alpha gorilla.

I'd dreamed of a woman the whole time. My ideal woman. Five-four, 36-24-36, cooks with a baby blue apron on — and only that, if you know what I mean — good cook, brunette, long hair, maybe Italian, gives good head, a co-conspirator in my scheme to rule the world, just our world, you know, nothing big. A strong but loving mother. My first mate on the ship of life.

I never saw the shit stains or the kicked-in robot chassis. Even as I panicked from Coconut's hug, I warmed inside because it felt like love.

I found my center. I calmed, just a little. "You don't need my money. You get the basic income and you have your corporate gig. Come on."

She turned her back to me. "Someone needs to teach you a lesson. To stand up for women everywhere." She turned around, her face like an overused bath scrub. "I deserve a good man. A man with the smile of Tom Cruise, the body of Arnold Schwarzenegger and the altruism of Ryan Gosling in *Drive*."

"Look, baby, it's just that you're hitting the wall. I mean, next week is your 28th birth—"

"And you're not giving it to me! Get out! Before I call the Femforcers on you."

I knew how these things went down. There was no saving it now. I'd give her a week to cool off. She'd miss me. I'd get her to delay her claim on my assets. Push it back a week, a month and the clock might just run out. In three years.

Or I could withdraw the limit every day and I might just save some of it.

I grabbed my shirt and stepped into my shoes. I pulled my trusty Google Men® backpack from behind the washing machine. It was all in there — my ID, my release papers, a change of clothes and Dad's Victorinox Night Vision watch.

I could go. Dad, the forest up north. Just another runaway man. I'd be out of their hair. They wouldn't care.

"That's it! I'm calling the Femforcers!" She reached for the phone.

I flung open the door and flew down the curved steps. I grabbed the metal handle and turned it. It wouldn't budge. She was blabbering now, her voice taking on that righteous Elizabeth-Warren tone. This was my chance and a damned door lock was blowing it. She'd never trusted me with the keys.

"Hey, baby, the door is locked! Can you come unlock—"

The top step creaked.

My skin crawled and a chill ran up my back.

"Just you wait there."

Bitch. Oh I knew better than to say it. I'd get myself a week in the hole for that. I threw my shoulder against the door. A deep ache ran through my back and to my heart. There was no give.

***

Three Femforcer buggies showed up for my extraction. Round-topped pink four-doors. The seats were wide but there was no legroom, especially in the back.

Six of them, three tight-shirted roly-polies, two buzz-cut butches and an emo girl in a pink tutu that was almost acceptably good-looking, if not for the permanent stinkface.

I got stuck with two butterballs. They stank of salami and sewage. Unwashed hair. No makeup. Little hairs grew around their mouths.

My stomach turned.

An orange and white tomcat sat in a birdcage next to me. He rolled over on his back. Adopt me, the poor guy said. Get me away from these nutty bitches!

The silent motor came on and the car vibrated lopsidedly. I was pushed higher as the second Femforcer got in, like a toddler raised up on a seesaw when his obese grandma plopped down on the other side.

I pulled out my phone and teleported to another world. I brought up FaceSmash and found a photo of Emmeline. That one where I wanted to take a good picture of her, to capture her beauty, but she was upset about not getting that promotion.

At the top, I typed in, "Pulls you out of Broseg." At the bottom, I typed, "Takes all your $$ and calls the Femforcers." I published it and put my phone away.

The buggy hit a pothole. The flab on the Femforcers rose and convulsed. The tomcat stuck a paw through the cage and scratched me.

Poor guy.

***

The bars clanged shut behind me. Broseg genpop. Broseg because it was male-only, secure housing. Never mind that it used to be a prison. Those emptied out fast after they decrimed drugs and passed the basic income. Corrections Corporation of America needed a new line of business and housing penniless unmarried men was just the thing.

"Nick!" A chunky arm floated in the air ahead of me like an inflatable man in a hurricane. He waddled up to me and we slapped hands.

"We've got the DAC going, bro. Dank memes at ten thousand an hour!"

"I'm just not in the mood." My chest hung heavy and my neck was tighter than Emmeline's you-know-what. I had to get some rest. Six months of trying to satisfy her took its toll.

Larry grabbed my arm. "No, seriously, you gotta see this. We actually programmed the DAC to search out and respond to Femforcer threads with manly memes. You won't believe some of these girls' responses."

I stopped and narrowed my eyes. "Setting aside the question of why this isn't a waste of your time and mine, don't you need to pay the DAC to get it to do this?"

"Yeah, we—"

Maddox and Jeff trotted over. The former my big bro, the latter an old bud from high school, I hung out with them because they relieved my boredom and isolation.

"No, look guys." I took a step backwards. "Seriously, I have to get some rest."

But they grabbed my arms and dragged me in. The struggle against women continued.

***

"I really owe you. Thanks." I made my best sad-grateful face with my trademarked pout and lowered brows. I don't think it worked.

"Yes, you do. I expect you to eat out twice per day and a solid lay at least three times a week. You don't come until I do! You'll clean the house every Saturday and sweep the kitchen clean every night. Are we clear?"

Hanna was tired. Some rubbish job kept her stressed out. Make-work tracking robots for maintenance. A bot should be doing it. But she was a strong, independent woman and strong, independent women worked. They had jobs, responsibilities, important ones. The world might spin off its axis if not for strong, independent women pushing against the collapsing pillars of society!

At least she wasn't a roly-poly. She kept her black hair shoulder length. She smelled alright.

The car stopped. Horns beeped behind us.

"I said, are we clear?"

"Yes, of course!"

"Repeat it back to me and make it quick." She engaged the parking brake with a crunch and I put a protective hand over my groin.

I rolled up my window. A car screamed past us on the left, a fattie giving us the finger.

"Repeat it!"

"Oral twice per day, a good lay three times per week—"

"Or more! If you want it…"

"Cleaning once per week—"

She disengaged the brake and hit the gas pedal. Another car tried to pass us on the left and our fenders came within millimeters. I exhaled. My chest ached. They say you can't have a heart attack at twenty-five, but I was about ready.

"I'm sorry. It's just been so stressful lately and I haven't had a man in my life since…"

"Five years?"

"Four months, three weeks, two days and a couple of hours." She laughed out loud. I loved that laugh, it was like the uncorking of a champagne bottle. Pure joy. It was under pressure. It needed to get out.

I grabbed her hand and rubbed my thumb under her knuckles. She was getting chubby, that way girls bulk up when they stress-munch too many carbs. It was ugly. "I'm going to cook for you."

"Really!" She shot me that toothy grin of hers and I fell back through time. Things were so good between us. What went wrong?

"As soon as we get in, can we just go to bed. I'm shaved. I've got the wine you like chilled and you can get started while I take a quick—" Her phone strummed like an angry guitar and she tapped her ear to answer.

Her face turned dark and she looked at me.

"Understood, ma'am, but I just need an hour— Yes, of course. It's just—" She hung up.

I waited in silence, not sure if I should speak or pop the door and throw myself out into the brush. We zipped by a little forest. I could dive out, limp over there, climb a tree and they wouldn't find me for at least a half hour.

"So you posted something about your ex?"

"That? I know it was a bad idea but it was the heat of the—"

"The Femforcers have deemed it a sexist meme. There's an APB out for you. I'm supposed to bring you in." She pulled the car over, jammed the emergency brake into place and slid down into the seat. "Five years, Nick. Can you even imagine how I feel!"

"They put out an APB... for a meme?"

"I'm talking about my feelings here, Nick! Jesus, you are emo-deaf. I'm so oppressed right now!"

Now I remember why it didn't work out. "We'll go to a hotel. They won't find us there."

"I'll have to check in under *my* name, Nick. And they know I'm with you. God, you are so dense! You ruined this! You ruined my special day! You ruined your second chance. I don't give second chances, Nick!"

"I ruined this? Do you know what kind of torture— Screw this." I popped the door and put my foot on the soft gravel slope just past the ragged edge of the blacktop. My foot slipped, my back slammed into the rocks and my head cracked on the foot guard. I slid into a watery ditch.

She punched the accelerator and a cloud of dust and rocks fell into my open mouth.

I wanted to scream. I wanted to cry and complain but I pushed all that away. I was a man and the Femforcers were hot on my trail. Hanna probably already snitched on me.

I was a mess. I wouldn't make it far. But it was getting

dark. I picked my leg up and it wouldn't come. Mud. I reached up to get leverage. I burrowed my hand into the rock and dirt. I pulled. My left leg came out, encased in muck. But my right leg sank deeper.

Sweat poured down my forehead and over my eyes. The other side of the pit rose even higher. A thin root was my only hope. I secured my phone in my teeth and fell forward.

One hand landed on the root strand and my phone-filled mouth hung just millimeters from the murky liquid. Something shiny and dark jumped and skidded off my pants.

I could swear it was trying to get inside my jeans. I shook it off and pulled. I freed my foot and climbed up the embankment, one foot rising, then plunging even lower in the soft, wet dirt.

I got to the top, dirt jammed in under my fingernails, my pants heavy from the water and mud, my front a sticky mess, my whole being perfumed with the foulness of some dead animal. Who knows how long he was in that hole or how deep. No one was coming to bury him.

Police sirens raced toward me. Cars slowed. People pointed. I trudged into the forest.

I found a nice solid trunk and reclined. The moss below my butt was soft but the wind picked up and I chilled. A tremor ran through me. I wanted nothing more than a warm bed with the closest roly-poly.

I pulled my phone out of my teeth and brought up FaceSmash.

Holy fem-meltdowns.

"We know your name and we have your face. We're coming for you, you cis-white scum. You're shit. We're going to cut off your little buddy. We're going to stuff it and hang it on the wall at Femforcer Central."

I swallowed.

"His name is Nick Chesterton and he lives in Broseg No. 34 because his girl just dumped him for failure to satisfy. He has ED, a micro-dick and whines in his sleep. Pull him out under girlfriend pretenses, then rape and murder him. The world needs another example of fempower."

I rubbed my forehead. This was getting out of hand now. I scrolled down. There were dozens, maybe hundreds more like it.

An alert jumped onto my screen. "Your account is permanently banned for misogyny and hate speech. Go die in a fire. — FaceSmash Safe Speech Team."

I read the words over and over again. Go. Die. In. A. Fire. They wouldn't fit in my mind. I couldn't figure it out.

I looked back at the road, my head unsteady on my shoulders, my mouth panting of its own accord. Two cop cars leered at me. They blocked the road on both sides. Thin men in blue suits stood behind the cruisers, guns drawn. One pulled out a megaphone.

I tried to stand up. My legs denied me access. Like a total newb, I'd let them cool. Now they were numb. I grabbed the trunk and pulled my body up. I lumbered off, away from the forest and the cops, their megaphone droning in the distance behind me, the words garbled beyond recognition.

Up ahead a high, concrete fence blocked my path. I put my ear against it. It might be a housing development. There might be an empty house or someone who'd take me in.

My phone rang. "Yo."

"Dude, have you even seen—" It was Larry.

"Yeah, I'm public enemy number one. I need a place to stay. Know anyone around here?" I punched up my coordinates and sent them to him.

"Dude, you are public enemy number one, man. What the hell were you thinking?"

I clenched my teeth. I wanted to scream. With friends like Larry, who needed ignorant boobs to ask stupid questions at life-or-death moments?

"Oh, right, yeah, Maddox is looking that up for you. Hey, did you see the reaction from these African girls? They love you, man."

"What African girls?" The sun fell behind the mountains and a twilight gloom enveloped the world. Crickets chirped and something rustled in the forest. I ran around the corner and waited, my eyes on the trees.

"Maddox is sending you the link. Dude, you're like a celebrity now in this place, what is it? Er-rat-try-uh, thanks man. Dude, ever heard of Er-rat-try-uh?"

"You mean Eritrea? Isn't there a war going on there?"

"Whatever. Just read it." He cut the connection.

I found his message and brought up the link. Eritrean Women Love America's Most Sexist Man, the headline read.

Most sexist man? I posted one meme. One lousy meme

and I'm the most sexist?

I scanned the rest of the article. Desperate Eritrean women have lost all their good men to the war with Somalia and the South Sudan Jihadis. They want me to come visit them and take home a bride. Or two.

I dialed Larry. "This is a stupid joke. Where'd you get this? *Derfhole?*"

"I swear, it's—"

A sharp screech replaced Larry's voice and my phone went dead.

"We know you're in there! Come out with your hands up and your fly zipped!"

***

"So are you going?"

"Eritrea? Are you kidding me?"

I had a new phone, a kiddie job I picked up at the A-to-Z for four of my last seven bucks.

"Are you going to surrender?" There was that high pitch that came out in Larry's voice when he got tense.

"Listen, I got this. You just worry about getting yourself out of Broseg. Drop the pounds. Stick with the diet. You do your cardio yesterday?"

"Aw man, I for—"

"Don't even start. You want out? Drop the pounds."

"But what about—"

"Just do your cardio. You're getting too comfortable in there." I cut the connection and looked up at home. Well, mom's house. A squat, pink rowhome on a run-down city block. She was a lesbian now. That's what the *Times* article on her girlfriend said. Wife now.

I strode up the concrete steps from the sidewalk. It was dark inside and I started to shiver. I had that dry, hollowed out feeling after a night on the street, running from the cops.

They'd painted the door black but that smell remained, like spring showers mixed with motor oil and burning cookies.

I shouldn't be here. I turned and stopped myself. Where would I go? Nowhere. Fast. I turned back around and mustered all my strength. I knocked.

Feet thudded from far away like the approach of falling bombs. The door swung open.

"What do you want?"

The beast that faced me was unlike any woman I'd laid eyes on before. Brittle gray hair fell in straight lines around the wrinkled mush face of a centenarian. Sloppy breasts fell to her waist. I couldn't. I looked away.

"Oh! Nick?" She grunted. "Whatsamatter? Haven't seen breasts before? You're not a little boy anymore, you know." She grabbed my arm and pulled me inside with the strength of a butcher. The door slammed behind me.

"Is my mom around?" The house looked the same. A half-dozen cats lounged around on the backs of sofas and the tops of bookcases filled with female action figures and tiny porcelain penises. Tumbleweeds of cat hair floated on the scuffed hardwood floor. The Xmas tree was still up but it seemed to have more matted hair of indeterminate species than actual tinsel.

The top of the stairs creaked. "What are you doing here? Knocked up some girl? Looking for money? Well, I ain't got none."

"Don't be so hard on him." My mom's wife laid an arm over my shoulder and pressed her boobs into me.

"I just need a place for—"

"No. Get outta here. Femforcers already been on the phone to me three times this morning."

I turned to leave but I had to know. "Did you turn me in, Mom?"

The stairs creaked and she was gone. I threw open the front door, turned left and jumped down to the sidewalk. I ran three blocks straight down, past trees growing out of cracked pavement, angry mama pit bulls and round old men watering their concrete gardens.

I found a quiet alley and installed myself behind a green dumpster. My lungs expanded and contracted under their own control as if I was on a ventilator. No options. No way out but through the Femforcers.

My muscles ached, my lungs burned and my stomach growled. But new vigor coursed through my arteries. The air tasted of freedom and ideas for my newfound liberty flashed through my mind. I smiled despite myself. Running from Femforcers was a lot more fun than listening to Larry whining.

My phone buzzed and a message popped up. "You're surrounded. Come in now and we will only send you to sexcamp for six weeks. — The Femforcers LLC."

Sexcamp! The only place where you're guaranteed zero sex. These Orwellian bitches!

Another message pushed down the first. "Hello darling Nick! I am Fnan from Asmara, the capital city of Eritrea. On behalf of the Eligible Spinsters of Eritrea, we invite you to visit our fine country on holiday, all expenses paid, so that you might meet our lovely girls and perhaps select a devoted bride or two. Or even three. Your tickets await you at the African Airlines counter at the airport. We hope to see you soon!"

***

"I thought it would be hotter."

"I'm actually kind of cold." The corrugated sheet metal awning partially blocked my view of the sky. A lazy gray cloud drifted in front of the sun. A horse-drawn buggy passed by, carrying a load of scrap metal. Probably to be melted down into bullets. Or AK-47s. A rat-tat-tat echoed in the distance, maybe in the hills surrounding Asmara. It was far enough away I wasn't worried.

My brother set down his fork and sat up straight, his eyes wide. "Was that gunfire? Again?"

I grinned. "Relax. It's not near." I ripped off a piece of soggy flatbread and scooped up the last dribbling of a surprisingly tasty yellow paste. I chugged a bottle of Nestle mineral water and examined the label. No way this was the real thing. Some cheap knockoff, for all I knew it was radioactive goat bile. Faintly tasted like it, too.

"Made a choice yet? That Fnan is pretty cute. Final day." He snapped up the last chunks of mystery meat, mopped up the remaining crimson paste and disappeared it into his mug.

"Seven women have convinced themselves I plan to marry them. It's insane." I sat back against the hard wooden chair and burped. It was a good trip. I didn't want to get married. But if I turned down all these women, it was back home. The Femforcers were waiting and I faced up to three years in sexcamp.

Maddox downed his coffee, scraped his seat against the cement floor and walked out into the sun. A cinnamon-skinned woman with a baby blue hijab stopped and smiled at him. It was a great smile.

Three more approached me, their hands out, their heads wrapped in a delicate salmon fabric, their lips painted red and their eyes surrounded by pink makeup. It was just too much.

"Come to our house, we will feed you."

I ran. I ditched my bro. I pushed through a curtain. I stepped around the cook, the stink of blood and guts stewing in the tiny space over an open charcoal fire. I stepped out into the sun and looked up at the scrub mountain. Jeeps and tanks circled each other and the rat-tat-tat of the AK-47s echoed like breaking glass across the valley.

This was crazy. It was a stupid idea. And now three years of sexcamp awaited me.

I ran behind the brick buildings and shacks, turned right

through a meat market and found the main street. Women came from nowhere and everywhere.

"Nick! Wait!" A gaggle of women crowded around Maddox. He was gone.

I ran down the short block and turned left. My hotel towered at the end, like a Cinderella castle.

A jeep turned onto the street and I stopped. A dozen armed men sprouted from the vehicle at all angles, dressed in tan, pine green and chocolate brown camouflage with little black berets. It accelerated, then screeched to a stop in front of me.

The soldier in the passenger seat stood up and pointed at me. "You! Nick, they call you?"

I nodded. The buildings were wall to wall here. No exit.

"You marry Eritrean woman, then you join us in fight against Moo-slem invaders. Understand? You are in my unit. Elite!"

I nodded. Join the army? Fight Jihadis? What the hell had I gotten myself into?

"Let me hear you say it. 'Yes, suh.'" He gestured with his bone-thin arms and shook his curved rifle in the air.

"Yes, sir," I mumbled.

"Louder! Or the battle begins now." He pointed the rifle at me and charged a round.

The world spun a little. Was this really happening? Was I in a video game. I examined the graphics on the soldier's face. Too good for 8K. "YES, SIR!"

"Good, now get out of my way." The jeep blasted past me and I was left sucking up biofuel fumes.

"Hey, bro, wait up!"

Maddox ran toward me, at least fifty women short-step trotting along behind him, their ankle-length, skin tight dresses stretching and revealing. I sprinted into the hotel, found the elevator and jammed my index finger into the number twenty-four. Women poured into the lobby. The door closed. I leaned against the back wall and wheezed.

"I see you are very popular." The tone was honey, the rhythm like a soft morning bird call.

I opened my eyes and looked to my left, my jaw at my groin. Raven hair, smoothed straight back. Emerald green eyes behind curvy eyelids. Baby blue dress from neck to toe. She was small. I did the math. About five-four. Thin but with hips and ample bosom. If she wasn't 36-24-36, she was Godblessedly close!

"Hi!" My mouth went dry.

Her smile radiated excitement and embarrassment. If she'd been whiter, her flushed face would have been painfully obvious. She offered me her hand. "I'm Fatima. What's your name?"

"Nick. You're... You're—" Hold on, I told myself. Don't compliment her. It's the surest way to screw it up. Say something funny, ask her something interesting. Just say something!

The elevator pinged and the door opened.

She stepped forward, then turned and looked at me over her shoulder. My lungs seized up and junior rustled below. My tongue moved but no air passed over it.

"Bye, Nick!"

A fat, old black man in camouflage strode towards her

and grabbed her arm. "The general has been waiting five minutes for you. Do not forget your place, slave!" The crack from his slap actually made me jump.

She looked back at me and the elevator doors closed.

***

"Just keep an eye for any military."

"Hey, I got my own girl waiting." Maddox snapped his fingers.

"You actually picked just one?"

He made an angry face, the kind that means I better shut up or he's going to shut me up. That was a privilege big brothers had. They got to use credible threats of violence to get their way. But today was different.

"Invite her over. She can play lookout too."

I headed towards the back of the restaurant and nodded at the chef. He shot me a bright white smile and gestured at the table.

That's what a C-note bought you in Asmara, Eritrea — a private dinner date with the Supreme Leader of the Eritrean Army's captured Muslim slave girl. Right next to the boiling sheep soup and the bled-out pig.

But would she show?

I surveyed the two chairs. One rocked back and forth on uneven legs. The other looked like it was a sacrificial altar for sheep. I took the sacrificial altar and waited.

And waited.

I'd found her an hour later in the lobby, after our

elevator rendezvous. She'd lost her radiance. Her dress was ripped.

"Are you really a slave?" I'd asked her.

Her face told me everything.

"What if I could take you away from here?" Going around saving Muslim slave girls was not my thing. Ask anybody I know and they'd look at you like you were speaking Afghani. I mind my own business. I even go to church sometimes.

She said nothing but her mask came down and that sad-happy pout melted my heart.

She was the girl for me. It was an ugly world. You couldn't expect perfection anymore. She was still young. I don't know why, okay? We had chemistry. Every skin cell trembled around her. The heart wants what it wants, alright? Get off my back.

And then I told her where to meet me.

Breaking a slave out of Africa was new territory for me. I couldn't afford to risk it unless I knew she was the one.

The curtain fluttered and there she stood, a well-shapen hip cocked to one side, a mischievous lopsided grin on her face and the tip of her engorged tongue tickling her luscious lips.

I motioned for her to sit down and nodded to the chef. He grinned and set to serving. My stomach fluttered and spasmed.

"So, you want to rescue me, eh? Are you my knight in shining armor?" She giggled.

My eyes went wide and I sighed. Her blemish-free, copper skin. Her long, black hair. Those sharp brows, curvy eyes and strong cheeks.

I was smitten.

But common sense had to make an appearance, no matter how brief. I leaned in. "Do you want to be rescued?"

"You don't know anything about me. Maybe you just want to make me *your* slave?"

The food arrived, an oversized metal disk covered in flatbread with piles of yellow, black and crimson pastes and stews. She ripped off a hearty chunk of bread and dug in.

"Do you *want* to be my slave?"

"All you have are questions. Why are you so interested in me?" She shoveled a lamb stew in one hand and some hummus in another.

How much do I tell her? Do I bare my soul? The standard answer was: never!

But this was a Muslim slave girl in Eritrea in the middle of a war on my last night. It was now or never. Make the play for my dream girl or suck it forever.

I took a drink of Nestle mineral water and looked at the ceiling. "I've met at least five hundred girls here in Eritrea." I met her eyes and she met mine. "I know lots of girls back home. But none of them are as feminine as you. You're my dream girl. You're the right shape, the right height. You're gorgeous. You're beautiful. So beautiful." I gestured to her face and her chest. My face heated up and I fanned myself.

She leaned forward and laughed, her mouth open. She hid her eyes from me. I'd made an impression. This might just work.

"I want to take you with me. I'm leaving here tomorrow

morning and you're coming with me. If you want."

She looked back at me. She squinted and wiped her cheeks. "They burned my papers in front of me. I could sneak out only because the general is busy defending the capital. I can't go." She moved to get up.

"Wait." I grabbed her hand and held it. "I don't want you to go back to him."

"He is the top general in Eritrea. His soldiers will stop us no matter where we go!"

"Do you like me?"

Her face softened and she smiled. "Do you want children?"

"Now who's only asking questions?" I leaned in. Like I said, dude, it's all or nothing.

She leaned towards me and I caressed her lips with mine. Angels danced around me. My heart zipped and my groin sparked. Oh, this was it.

I stood up and grabbed her hand then sat back down and rearranged junior. I stood up again and pulled her out through the dining room.

"We're going. I don't care how. We're leaving."

We stepped outside and five hundred camera flashes discharged at once.

***

"How did you guys even get here?"

"We paid those hookers to check us out."

I wanted to stand up but they'd tied me to a chair in my

hotel room. Maddox, Larry and Jeff reclined on the couch in front of me, their pot bellies sticking out from under their faded t-shirts, beers in their hands.

"Hey, where is Fatima? And why am I tied to this chair!" I jerked my arms and legs. The chair creaked but nothing gave. For a bunch of losers, they sure know how to tie knots.

"I knew the boy scouts would be good for something, someday." Larry guffawed and the others laughed with him.

"Fatima's life is in danger. I could lose her forever. You need to—"

Larry stood up and dusted the crumbs off his belly. "There is no chance we are letting you marry one of these girls. That's why we came. Maddox said you were in trouble. You might remember the pledge we all made together a couple years ago. 'Men, going their own way, bros before hoes and I ain't getting married no how, no way!' Ring any bells, dude? We're getting you on that plane tomorrow morning, safe, sound and ring-free."

"Hey, boys, why don't you come and play?" A dull-skinned girl in a nurse's uniform stumbled out of the bedroom. Her face was smooth but the eyes were dead. Her head rotated to look at him, then stopped and bounced back and forth.

"Trixie is ready! Oh, yes!" Jeff stood up and wiggled his behind, his crack showing above his jean shorts.

"Guys, there are five hundred girls right outside. There are ten thousand more across this country who signed up to meet guys like us. And you went to the trouble of assembling that thing?" These guys were hopeless. I didn't even know what to say to them anymore.

Jeff burped. "Hell, no! This is the sixty-nine ninety. It self-assembles!" He trotted ahead and pinched the robot girl's butt.

It chirped a recorded giggle.

I wiggled in the chair again. No good. They tied my hands behind my back, my chest to the chair and even my knees and ankles. These guys weren't good at anything other than mass-producing Cheeto-scented farts and ableist knock-knock jokes. When the hell did they learn all this?

"Guys, I gotta get to this girl. She's a slave and she could be—"

"A slave?" Maddox stood up. "You fell in love with a slave girl? Don't tell me, you're going to rescue her. Oh my God, talk about white-knighting. What are we—"

A low rumble started below us and then a great chatter like a million rattlesnakes whispering to each other. The door burst open and in poured women: teenagers, twenty-somethings and over-forty cougars wearing leopard-spot tights. Short hair, long hair, frizzy curls and straight locks, chocolate brown, almost-white and everything in between.

They descended on me, their painted fingernails reaching, their red-lipped mouths moving.

***

"I want to cut off his balls! And make soup with them."

"I agree, Lindy, but this needs to be democratic."

I cracked my eye. I tried to move but my arms and legs

were tied down to the bed. My range of vision extended only to the ceiling and a tiny sliver of the living area. I wanted to ask them if I got a vote, too, but I knew the answer and I needed the element of surprise.

"We can get those other guys, too. Who knows how many of these poor African girls they've pumped and dumped already. I hate them! I hate them! All men should die!"

More voices joined in, whispering in harsh tones, not unlike that snake sound I'd heard before. I hoped the guys were alright. I really did.

Because I needed them to get me out of this!

The sharp shing of a knife being drawn and my body went as rigid as a three-day-old corpse.

"Guys, I think we should take turns with him first. I'm just saying... I don't know about you, but I have needs. Real, strong needs and this guy is pretty hot. So, yeah."

A burst of chatter erupted as they all blabbered at once. It was the kind of noise that would cover my escape. If only I could get free. I rocked back and forth.

The chatter stopped.

"Did you hear that? I think he's trying to escape!" Lindy yelled.

The chatter began again, lower this time. A girl appeared in the doorway.

"Who do you think you are anyway? The white man who's going to ride in on your high horse and save all these people? You can't do anything for them."

I blinked a dozen times, looked away and looked back. It

176

was really her. "Hanna, why did you come here?" I tried to sit up and the ropes cut deeper into my forehead, neck and chest.

Her face got tight and she bit her lip. "What are *you* doing here? You need to come back with me."

"What about your friends? Is there gonna be anything left to go back to? Cut me free."

She crossed her arms and shook her head. "This is for your own good."

I summoned my most genuine face. The fate of my boys hung in the balance. "I want to go home, with you. Cut me loose and we can go."

She nodded and stepped forward.

The chattering stopped and heavy footsteps landed outside. Hanna fell into the wall and a new, wider presence blocked my view.

"Oh, you're not going anywhere. Not until we fix you." One lazy eye looked to my left and I struggled to decide which one to focus on.

Hanna stood back up. "He's my boyfriend, Lindy. We just got back together. Hands off!" She pushed the roly-poly but bounced back into the wall.

Lindy produced a knife and was on the bed. The ropes loosened a little and I fell towards the foot of the bed. She unbuckled my pants and I couldn't help myself. Junior grew up.

I searched for anything, any thought, no matter how horrid — poop, old men, the smell of liverwurst, anything — but he kept growing. A rough hand pulled down my underwear and he popped free, towering above my spread-eagled body like a flag pole over a conquered nation.

Icy, cold hardness touched me down there and I startled.

Lindy laughed and looked back at the other girls. "He's a pussy. He's not a real man."

I lifted up my head. "Which of you is making my sandwich? I want ham on rye with Swiss cheese, Batavia lettuce, one slice of beefsteak tomato and some Dijon mustard. You know what, I'm hungry. Make that two sandwiches and a six pack of Red Stripe. And get something for yourselves."

Lindy leaned forward, a new light in her face. She nuzzled her nose against junior.

For a split second I doubted myself. Then the girls stampeded for the door and slammed it behind them.

I lay back down and focused on my breathing. Girls. This shit always worked, everywhere, in any situation. I wanted to put my hands behind my head and gloat but I still had a problem.

The front door clicked and Lindy appeared, a little green pairing knife in her hand.

"You don't think I'm that stupid, do you?"

***

I found a point on the wall and fixed my eyes on it.

Lindy was jerking her hips in a depraved striptease. It reminded me of an elephant I'd once seen on the Discovery Channel that was winging its butt hither and fro trying to get a tiger to unbuckle its teeth from his ass.

The sound of stampeding bulls came from far away coupled with the rat-tat-tat of gunfire.

Lindy's eyes went wide and she pulled at her pants. Her belly flopped over the top of them like a yeast culture overgrowing its petri dish at 32x playback.

The outside door slammed into the wall and something cracked. Eritrean girls — some I recognized — poured into the room. Fnan kicked Lindy into an armchair that promptly buckled and snapped.

Chinese soldiers in gray camo and little red hats with a single yellow star each trailed after the women like bored kids on a clothes shopping trip with mom. One walked up, saluted me with a snap of his heels and pulled an eight-inch, black-handled Bowie knife from his gun belt. He held it up in front of his face and grinned at me.

I tried to scurry away.

Fnan grabbed my hand and I swiveled to face her. "Don't worry, Mr. Nick, these men are Chinese Army, our allies." She bowed to me and grinned like she'd just hooked a prize fish.

"Fnan, thank you for riding to my rescue. But I have to find someone and—"

Maddox burst into the room. "Oh my God, bro, you have no idea what we just went through looking for you."

I shook my head and rolled my eyes at him. Fnan extended her arms and I hugged her, her long hair sticking in my mouth. She retracted and looked at me, expecting something more. She wanted me. Hell, this was the girl who invited me to Eritrea in the first place. She lobbied the government to pay our expenses.

"Have you selected the girl you wish to marry?"

I opened my mouth. How would I break the bad news to her without getting a Chinese slug in the cerebellum? A hand landed on my shoulder. I turned and one of the soldiers bowed to me.

"Please, sir, Nick…" His accent was thicker than frozen sweet-and-sour sauce. "Your flight leaves in…" He pulled back his velcro-tightened sleeve to reveal an oversized black watch. "…twelve hours. We need to make the arrangements for your wedding."

I looked back at Fnan then stepped in closer to the soldier and whispered, "What if she's a slave?"

His head jerked down and bounced back and forth. "Slave?"

I cringed. "Shh. Yes."

"Ehhhh. Mmmmm. Slave girl? No, no, no. It must be an Eritrean girl over the age of fourteen, sir Nick. And please, hurry up. The girls are on strike unless more real men like you come to the country and marry." He poked me in the chest and grinned. "You and your friends give them hope. Because all their men dead or dying from war."

It hit me like a ton of lipstick cartridges. I wasn't getting out of Africa alive unless I got married. *Tonight.* Fnan giggled and the soldier smiled.

***

"It's called thalassophobia."

"What? You're so silly." Fnan had struck sexy paydirt in her tight-fitting, plunging-neckline pearl wedding dress. Simple but classy, her more than adequate curves stood out in sharp relief. Her curled hair framed a girlish, bronzed face and brown eyes that any man could contemplate for hours at a stretch.

But I wasn't any man. I wanted Fatima. Maybe it was stupid, maybe it was self-destructive but I didn't want the safe choice, the solid girl, the regular woman.

I wanted a hot, sexy chick that lit my fire and kept it stoked all night!

"You're smart, Fnan." I wagged my finger at her. "Bring me out to sea in a boat, at night. Where do I go? It's just shark-infested ocean. The shore is barely even lit up." I looked back. If I jumped now at least I would be pointed in the right direction.

Or maybe I'd get turned around and not see the shore over the waves. I could end up in Yemen, if not the gullet of a hammerhead shark.

She put her arms around my neck and pulled me close. "Don't worry. I always dreamed of getting married on the water. Isn't it nice? And look, my father, the general, will marry us."

From behind her, a pot-bellied man with sunglasses and a chest of medals sauntered out of the darkness. Fatima stood a step behind him to his left. She glanced at me, fiddled with her dress and looked down again.

The general reached a hand to her butt and pushed her

forward. "You like, eh?"

Fnan's face fell.

He took off his glasses. White eyes boiled in the blackness of his skin. "She is mine. I put a bullet through her father's head and no man may take her except through battle." He pulled a black pistol from his belt and pointed it at me.

"Father!"

I laughed. It was just too ridiculous. Two weeks ago, I was a kept man and lacked nothing but a little peace. Now, I was facing marriage to a strange woman, a bullet, a watery grave and being recycled into shark poop. I drew breath and laughed harder.

Fnan relaxed. The general closed his eyes, threw back his head and guffawed, his gun pointed at the sky.

It was all the chance I needed.

I darted at Fatima. I grabbed her hand and pulled her over the side of the boat.

A woman screamed. Gunshots rang out. Something heavy hit my head and it all went black.

***

"Don't worry, I have a plan."

"Do you have any cigarettes?"

I raised an eyebrow. She smokes? I don't even *date* girls who smoke. She was gorgeous, despite being all wet, her hair a disaster, her green dress in tatters and her thin legs bruised. I loved her more as a hot mess.

Humid, sandy and salty, everything was sticky, and not

in a good way. We had to go to Djibouti, the tiny nation just south of this tiny nation. I liked the sound of that because it ended in 'booty.'

Not that I had the energy for it right now. But it was the only thing keeping me going.

I don't know how we got to shore. She said she dragged me in but it seems impossible. In any case, it's not just love anymore. I really owe this girl.

I cupped her hand in mine. "Are you gonna make it?"

She gave me her strongest smile. "I'm really thirsty. And hungry. There should be a restaurant up ahead. And we need a car." Her clipped accent mesmerized me and I had to replay in my mind what she'd just said.

"How far is it?"

"At least five hundred kilometers."

Five hundred kilometers?

"And the general will be coming after me. He told you a lie. He did not win me in battle. I am from Pakistan and he purchased me at an auction in the South Sudan. In Eritrea, this is legal because of his position but in Djibouti, my freedom will be respected and I will be able to get my papers." She hugged me, her arms wrapping around my lower back, her salty-wet hair under my nose. "Will you help me?"

"Yes, yes, of course. I love—" I stopped myself. I got the distinct impression I was risking my life for a girl who just wanted to use me for her freedom. That may sound harmless but I'd bargained for something more.

"I love you, too." She looked up at me with those curvy eyes of hers.

"Really? I mean, like, what are— I mean…" I cleared my throat. Talk like a man! "I want us to get married. I want to take you with me to the US, or for us to live together, anywhere really."

She covered her mouth and giggled. "I want that, too."

I grabbed her hand and strode forward with the self-confidence of a thousand mustangs. There was the restaurant. We'd eat. We'd get on a bus or something and get to Djibouti. After a week in bed, we'd figure out the rest. I'd get a job as a—

A scream like a Godzilla-sized wounded eagle and the restaurant exploded into an orange ball. Range Rover windshields popped and Honda dirt bikes fell over. Rocks and dust plopped to the dusty ground around us. I held her tight, my back and head shielding her body from the fallout.

Another scream boomed behind us and a smaller explosion registered down the road. Troops in brown camo poured from ground zero on foot and in jeeps.

Behind us, a column of tanks squeaked down the road. Rifle-wielding, quick-marching troops in bold Eritrean camo followed in rows and columns, their boots smacking the dusty road in unison, with a crack that soaked my brain in adrenaline. A dozen gray, thin-beaked Chinese attack choppers zoomed in low and Fatima's dress flapped up to reveal plump butt cheeks.

"It's the general. We have to hide!"

She grabbed my arm and pulled me off the road. We ran across a plowed field of red soil and made for a giant sycamore tree. Like a goliath's green hat, discarded in the dirt, we huddled under it.

Shells landed not five hundred feet from us. I had to make my move. I pulled her tight and grabbed her generous behind.

"I want you now."

"But we're trapped. And we could die!"

"Love is a rebellion against death, baby."

She slammed her lips into mine. I pulled up her dress, pushed her panties to one side and went to heaven.

***

"What if they ask for my papers?"

"They won't. It won't come to that."

It'd better not. After three weeks aboard the *MV Ascension*, Fatima was undoubtedly with child. No internet, no TV, just sealing the deal morning, noon and night, condom-free. We dined on expired instant ramen bowls, took long romantic walks on deck and avoided the surly all-male crew.

A long strip of Caribbean highrises poked out of the ocean outside my porthole. Hello, Miami.

We were still unmarried. We had fifteen dollars and thirty-six cents left to our names. Neither of us had papers.

We had something better. We were compatible. Twenty-six days in the crucible that is a tiny cargo ship cabin proved that. We didn't hate each other. We didn't tire of the sex and we looked each other in the eye every single time we came. Which we did together, I might add.

This was Earth-shaking stuff. I was ready to slaughter Christians for her. I was declaring jihad on the world.

Because Fatima and I would live together forever in the forest with Dad, no matter what it took.

The door squeaked open and banged the wall. A buzz-cut old hag in a tan uniform stepped in. "US Immigration. Papers, please."

"Uh…" I pulled my pants on. "Yeah, they're in our other cabin."

"Hurry up and go get 'em. I don't have all day." She studied her clipboard.

I grabbed Fatima's hand and pushed into the hallway.

The immigration agent squeezed my wrist. "The girl stays here."

Well, there went my plan. It wasn't much of a plan but you can hardly blame me. I'd been a little busy the last three weeks.

A length of heavy pipe and one hit to the back of the head. No. Then they'd be looking for us and Captain Hong would be in for it. Fatima squeezes out the porthole and into the sea. No. She and the baby'd be crushed between the ship and the dock on the next wave.

I sauntered down the hall, in no particular hurry. Coming clean would mean months in an underground holding cell for Fatima. The baby'd be born down there and immediately placed for adoption. Who knew what kind of charges I'd get.

Good thing I had a backup plan. There it was. I pulled the red lever and the ship's horn and bells absorbed the known universe into their cacophony.

The immigration agent pushed past me, headed for the dock at breakneck speed. I grabbed our bag in one hand, gripped Fatima's hand in the other and let my pride flow out through my grin. But she was tense.

We sprinted in the opposite direction from the agent. We climbed narrow stairs, did a one-eighty and climbed more narrow stairs. This became our life for a full five minutes until we were gasping for air like fish out of water and I was certain the immigration agent had called for backup.

We hit the deck and shuffled left. I lagged behind. Fatima was a real trooper. Or maybe she ached for her freedom more than I wanted mine. I couldn't be sure.

Hong helped us into the lifeboat, a size x-x-small yacht with a covered bridge. I took the newspaper-wrapped box he needed delivered and we hopped in.

"Remember, the Four Seasons 4PM today, side gray door. If you're not there, I have to give them your info to save my own neck."

I grabbed his hand and squeezed. "Thanks, man."

He raised his eyebrows and released the boat. We freefalled to the ocean forty feet below, splashed down and hit our heads on the ceiling.

Hong, you careless bastard! "You okay?"

She held her belly and looked up at the ceiling, then nodded, her face dark with worry.

I sparked the engine and jammed the throttle to full ahead. We zoomed away from the *Ascension*, past another huge cargo ship and then another. I turned left and we flew up a little inlet next to a sprawling gray warehouse. I ran the boat up onto shore. It rolled to one side and we jumped out.

The shadow of a helicopter fluttered next to us. We sprinted to the street, jumped onto a red and white city bus and found two seats.

***

"What are you going to do for money?"

"What do *you* do for money?"

I sliced off another chunk of green apple with my old boy scout knife and stuffed it into my mouth. Light, sweet and tart. Damn, that was good.

The pale yellow sun peaked above the pine-treed mountains to my right. Dad sat backwards in an old dining room chair to my left on the porch of his x-large Alaskan log cabin.

"So you're going to hunt, forage and farm with me? It's a hard life. Sometimes I work from before dawn to midnight and still I don't have all the calories I want. Is Fatima up for that?" He looked at his watch. "Can't usually sleep this late, definitely not in winter. You're going to need cash for formula—"

"She's going to breastfeed."

"You better get her trained up then. There's a midwife about ten miles to the South. You'll need cash for her. The last thing you want is a hungry newborn and Fatima's breasts not pumping."

My mind folded in on itself. "Is that really a thing?"

"Happened to your mother. I knew it could because happened to Auntie Irma. Took your mom to a midwife but she refused to try. Shelled out for months of formula, bottles, all that junk, for you. That's why you were sick so often."

I didn't know any of this stuff.

Dad laughed, that hearty one where he knew he knew more than you and was right but wasn't making a big deal out of it. A Buddha kind of laugh. Very zen. But without the flapping belly.

He twitched his mustache at me. "You really don't know what you're in for, do you? Having a kid is not like going to the store to pick up the latest video game. It's a big goddamned deal." He sighed and stood up. "Tell you what, fatherhood classes start today. You ready?"

I stood up and thrust out my chest. "Ready, Dad!"

"Lesson one, go make breakfast. Canadian bacon, eggs, pancakes and some of that smoked caribou sausage on the side for me. Make sure Fatima gets her prenatal vitamins, too. Doc Johannson will be asking about that."

I nodded in a manly fashion, turned and opened the screen door. The squeak distorted the sound of car tires on gravel. I stepped inside, pressed my back against the wall and held my breath.

The pink buggy jerked and flopped up to the porch. Two heavy girls in body armor and a third in a pink tutu popped out and gave each other nasty looks.

"Hello there, sir, we're midwives looking for work." The

driver approached the front step. It was goddamned Lindy.

I wanted to scream out to Dad, to attack those bitches and hand them off to the bear family up the mountain.

"You don't look like any midwives I've ever seen."

The dressed-in-all-black roly-poly behind Lindy sighed. "Lindy, dear, this is not going to work. Look, sir." She put her foot on the front step. "We're Femforcers and we know you're harboring fugitives. Turn them over and we won't have to mount a picket line or declare your land a safe space."

"A safe space?"

"We will issue a call to all good feminists within five-hundred miles to stop exploitation on your land, including hunting, trapping, animal husbandry, gardening—"

"Gardening?"

"Gardening is rape of Mother Earth." The words shot from the pink tutu girl's mouth like AK-47 gunfire.

"What?" Dad took a step back.

"You'll have to receive sensitivity and equality training and there'll be group therapy for you boys to release your burden of manhood, learn how to be vulnerable and share your feelings openly."

"And that's just the first six months." The second fattie scratched her butt and picked her nose.

"I want you off my land."

Lindy took another step up to the porch and the wood creaked like a bear in heat.

"We need to search your house. The police are just behind us."

"But," the second one piped up, "if you give us the boy, we'll tell the cops the woman isn't here and we'll move on."

"Neither of them are here."

The other two women put their full weight on the porch steps. All three oak slabs gave way and the trio landed on their behinds in the dirt.

"I think we have a case to sue, for damages, distress, emotional anguish. It's almost like he raped us. We'll turn this place into a Femforcer solidarity retreat," Lindy said.

It was just too much. I opened the screen door.

"I give up. Just leave my family alone."

***

"Mr. Chesterton, you face a single charge of hate speech, fleeing custody, exiting the jurisdiction without prior permission, unlawful entry, bondage slavery, aiding and abetting an illegal alien, rape after the fact and I have an extradition request from the Republic of Eritrea for theft of property and breach of marriage contract." The bald old judge looked down at me from his high perch over the tops of his bifocals. "Sounds like you had the meltdown of the century, young man. These are serious allegations and you're facing life in prison on the hate speech charge alone."

"Your honor, these charges are without merit and you have our motion to dismiss in front of you."

That was my lawyer. The guys in Broseg gathered their dimes and their old bottle caps together and with a little help from Men Going Their Own Way, Inc., this well-muscled blond guy showed up.

"Motion to dismiss denied."

My lawyer stood up. "Your honor, you haven't even read—"

"That's your first warning, Mr. Brotz. I will hold you in contempt if you keep it up."

"I apologize your honor, this is my first Twitter trial." My lawyer sat down.

"What do you mean, a 'Twitter trial?'" I looked past him at the prosecutor, a twenty-something brunette with a man's business haircut wearing a defense lawyer's Armani suit. Lindy overflowed the chair next to her. Behind them, all dozen rows of benches were taken up by overweight women wearing the pink and yellow Femforcer sash.

Brotz put a hand between us and whispered, "It's a new thing the Femforcers are doing whereby the Twitter community is the jury. The court is livestreaming the trial. Twits discuss it live and at the end, there is a straight up and down, guilty or not guilty vote that any previously verified twit can participate in. Except you and I, of course."

"Why can't we vote?"

"Conflict of interest."

I looked for the windows. Then the air vents. I couldn't find them. It was hot in here, too hot. "This is crazy. I need some air." I stood up.

Every Femforcer behind the prosecutor rose and looked at me. Brotz pulled me back down.

"You're in custody, Nick. Stepping outside for a breath of fresh air is an escape attempt. Now, relax. MGTOW, Inc.

is marshaling the men for the vote. And Larry is upgrading the DAC. We've got this. Just make sure to be honest in court, to speak your mind, because your radical meninism is what will motivate our guys to support you."

Meninism? "So I shouldn't try to tone anything down?"

"No."

The front of the judge's bench flickered. A screen came to life, taller than me and running its full-length, from the court reporter's station to the end of the witness stand.

Words fell down from nowhere.

"RageParty365: Boring! Where are the gallows?"

"FemForcerOfficial: I want to see him castrated. Live!"

"ShitLordSprayxx99: Can we just vote right now and erase this cis scum from the planet forever?"

"FatimaAndDad: We love you and are waiting for your return."

"HannaWantsBanana: @FatimaAndDad hold your breath and die in a fire bc he ain't coming home. Ever!"

I looked at Brotz and he looked away. The whole world fell on me and I wished I'd never existed.

***

"This is bullshit!"

"That's thirty days of sensitivity training at a sexcamp of the Femforcers' choosing, Mr. Chesterton, to run consecutively with whatever sentence the jury hands down for you."

This was no kangaroo court. It was a bounce house! The

Femforcers blathered on for hours about how my meme hurt their feelings and my escape from 'accountability' offended their concept of justice. But the judge barely allowed Brotz to object.

And now he was handing out months in sexcamp like condoms in a middle school.

I looked back at my brother and nodded.

"What if the jury finds me not guilty, your honor?"

"Unlikely," he mumbled. "Now, Mr. Brotz—"

"Excuse me, what did you say?"

"Mr. Brotz, do you wish to cross-examine this witness! And get your client under control." He banged his gavel.

Brotz grabbed my shoulder and pulled.

"They're railroading me here, man, you see that, too, right? It's like they're running a train on me, a legal train and I am just getting f—"

"Just stop." He grabbed my other shoulder and turned me to face him. "We're going to get this on appeal. We've got plenty of basis—"

"Appeal? No, no, no. You said you had this. How long does that take?"

"Mr. Brotz, you are trying my patience!" The judge banged his gavel again.

He looked up at the ceiling. "With the backlog, about ten years. Then a couple more to complete the process."

"Twelve years!"

"Ninety days in sexcamp, Mr. Chesterton and fifteen for you, Mr. Brotz, to begin immediately." The judge banged his gavel.

"You're taking my lawyer from me now?" This was insane. I'd caught a few episodes of *Matlock* and missed not one of *LAPD Judges*, but this was nothing like that! "Now, wait, your honor—"

The bailiff thumped her feet over and snagged Brotz's arm. She pulled him through the little swinging doors and past the leering Femforcers.

"Good luck, Nick!" Brotz shrugged.

"Fifteen-minute recess." The judge banged his gavel once more and disappeared.

The bailiff shot me a menacing look and I raised my hands in surrender.

Maddox appeared behind me. "Ask for a bathroom break and then climb out the bathroom window. Turn left and we'll be waiting."

I nodded.

Maddox retreated and I focused on the Twitter feed. It was ninety-nine percent racist sexist hate with the occasional love note from Fatima and every once in awhile a demand for marriage by some random post-wall tumblrina.

I stood up, found the bailiff and mouthed, "Bathroom break."

She firmed her jaw, tightened her eyes and nodded in a slow, angry bob.

I pushed through the swinging doors with tight little steps. My hands were free but the leg cuffs jingled with every midget stride.

I got into the hallway. I looked left, then right. A gaggle of Femforcers plodded towards me, like gnomes in sumo suits. I turned left.

There it was. The little white man running to freedom. Or to avoid soiling his pants. I turned left and headed straight to the end.

Just one short window, shaped like a 1950s TV set, promised release into another world. It hung above a ribbed radiator.

I put my hand on the radiator then whipped it back. Hot!

I tried to raise a foot onto the radiator but they were cuffed. I'd have to grab onto the windowsill and pull myself up without the benefit of my legs. I reached for it.

The door burst open behind me. Femforcers plodded in. Two grabbed my arms and pulled me down.

Lindy walked to the front of the passel and showed me her crooked, yellow teeth.

"Good news, Nick. Your girlfriend is arriving in five minutes to face some charges of her own. With both of you in a cage for the foreseeable future, I'm on the shortlist to adopt your kid."

***

"So, you see, members of the jury, I am just a humble man looking for true love, a hopeless romantic desperate for a chance at being a regular human guy. A man. With a woman. And kids. Everything I did," I said into the quadrotored camera lens, "I did in order to fulfill my—"

"Loser cis scum!"

I looked up at the judge. He'd fallen asleep again, a bead of saliva on the cusp of his lip.

"To fulfill my destiny as a man by serving a good woman with love—"

"An exploited brown underage trafficking victim from the third world!"

I looked back at the Femforcers. They sat in neat rows and columns in their creamy pink shirts with their arms crossed, like a jumbo box of heart-healthy eggs.

I looked down at my public defender. He was lost somewhere else. Didn't dare speak up against a woman. Not if he wanted to keep his crappy eighty-grand-a-year vocation.

"The highest law is love. And that's all I wanted, not duty or drudgery, not nagging or whining. Love and hot sex. And a quiet life in the woods with my dad and lots of kids. And that's what she wants too.

"I posted the meme that started all of this in a moment of desperation, something I'm sure all of you fine ladies out there can identify with." Damn. I shouldn't have said that. "But in the end, this is about freedom. I'm a human being, just like any lady, and I deserve the freedom to live outside of Broseg, on my own, without a woman sponsor—"

A great intake of breath came from behind me, like the sputtering of a thousand sperm whale blowholes.

"How dare you!" a Femforcer said.

"Next he'll want the right to travel freely!" another said.

"Men are beasts that require constant control to keep them from raping indiscriminately," yet another interjected.

"And to travel freely to other countries, marry and have children with any woman who voluntarily consents—"

"Monster!"

The Twitter feed exploded. Messages flew down so fast I could only catch the memes.

And they were all Sad Hitler now.

I sat down. No one was going to hear me over the pussy riot behind me. At this point, my only hope was the DAC. This wonder software had to date published precisely one tweet in support of me.

They'd better get the vote right.

"Your honor!" The androgynous prosecutor stood up and the judge startled awake. "If the defense rests…"

"Indeed. Move to penalty phase."

I banged my fist on the table. "Excuse me, I haven't been convicted yet."

"You will be."

"What?" Did he really say that?

"Sit down, defendant!" He banged his gavel and the wooden base flipped off and landed on the floor at my feet. He cocked an eyebrow.

I looked away. I wouldn't be a party to my own destruction. I wouldn't retrieve his little wooden disc. It wasn't a meaningful gesture, but it was all I had.

"If that's how you want it. Begin the voting." He stood up, lumbered down from his perch, got the disc and hmphed at me.

The screen flashed static, then black. Two words appeared: "Guilty" in red all-caps; and "Not Guilty" in green lowercase. Two zeros and a percentage sign appeared under each. The zeros spun like cherries in a slot machine.

The first numbers popped up. Sixty-nine percent guilty. I looked back at Maddox. His face was red and he was yelling into his phone.

Text appeared under the percentages.

"Probation: 5%"

"Death Penalty: 15%"

"Castration: 55%"

"Life in Sexcamp: 25%"

The public defender leaned in, whiskey and onions on his breath. "Keep in mind that any sentence over twenty percent will be binding upon you."

I sunk deep into my seat. I was a dead man. If they didn't do it, I would. Nobody was going to take my boys.

"How long does the voting—"

The judge banged his gavel. "Voting is now closed! Order in the court!"

I looked at the public defender. "Already?"

He stood up. "Your honor, we beg the court for mercy. This trial by Twitter is new and untested. Your honor has the power to set aside its verdict, at your—"

"Sit down. The defendant is found guilty of all charges. He will serve life in a sexcamp at the discretion of the Femforcers. And he will be castrated at the earliest possible moment." He fixed his stare upon me. "Mr. Chesterton, my only regret is that we fell three points short of the death penalty. Bailiff, remand the defendant into the custody of the Femforcers."

The world holds dangers for a man. Ten thousand years ago, a random saber-toothed tiger could take you out. Today, you might walk to the 7-Eleven, guzzle a couple sodas and burn your esophagus. Or the sedentary life of modern screencentric man could blow out your arteries.

But one threat has remained constant: women. Then, it was your own desire and the hungry, wailing babies it produced.

Today, women were the predators. And it was time someone — some *man* — took a stand.

Maddox was at my back. I reached and found cold steel. I settled the pistol grip into the webbing between thumb and forefinger. I pulled back the slide and pointed it at the judge, my arm a ramrod of death.

"Get over here!"

The judge stepped down from his bench and I grabbed him by the back of the neck.

"Please don't hurt me. I have a family." His upper lip trembled and his dark-circled eyes shot from side to side.

"So do I!" I pushed him ahead of me. Maddox, Larry and Dad pushed the Femforcers up against the wall, grunting like wildebeest as one coward stampeded the next.

The bailiff drew and I shot her.

"I was going to surrender." She fell to her knees, blood trickling from her arm.

"Where's Fatima?"

Dad shook his head at me.

We burst into the corridor.

"Dad, where is she?"

"The Femforcers have her. They say if you cooperate and serve your sentence, they'll release her into my custody. But if you don't, they'll abort the baby. They think she was raped and say the fetus is oppressing her."

***

"And then, he told the leader that if she dropped trou right there, he'd do her. And she did!"

"We know, Dad, we were all there."

"And then he kicked her plum in the—"

"Dad, enough!" I rolled my eyes and snuggled up against Fatima. I ran my hand over her tummy. Eight and a half months. She was big. Her back ached and she was eating ice cream by the gallon. But she was a trooper. Barely ever complained and still tried to cook and clean.

But I'd have none of it. It was strict bed rest for the foreseeable future.

"And then he rescued me." Fatima pecked me on the cheek and smiled at the group.

"But I do not understand. Why all of this big deal about love and sex?" Fnan sat on the long, green couch and gripped Maddox's beerless hand between her two palms. Next to them, Larry'd captured the mouth of Fatima's older sister Asma, and refused to let go.

"Love makes the world go around." I sighed. "And when you don't have love, that world has got to stop spinning. Plus, what else is there?"

Dad pried his hand from his fiancée's long black fingers

and looked at his watch. "Ladies and gentlemen, it's bedtime. Come on. We're building Jeff and Zewdi's house tomorrow and it needs to be move-innable by the end of the week."

I put my head on Fatima's shoulder and she leaned into me. It might be Alaska. Winter was coming and our cultures were barely compatible, but we had love, all of us. And with any luck, we'd keep having it, for the rest of our lives, damn the Femforcer blockade.

George Donnelly is the author of space opera, robot apocalypse and dystopian science fiction series. A rebel and unreformed idealist, he believes equally in human rights and abundant hugs before bedtime. Get a new free short story every month at georgedonnelly.com.

Want to Get Book 3 in the *There Will Be Liberty* Series for Free?

If you liked *Valiant, He Endured*, you'll LOVE *Intrepid, She Blasted*, the third book in the *There Will Be Liberty* anthology series, due out April 2017.

VISIT THE LINK AND CLAIM YOUR EBOOK, FREE.

GeorgeDonnelly.com/ISB

Thank you for reading!

Did You Like This Book?

WE NEED YOU...

Without reviews, indie books like this can't find their audience.

Leaving a review will only take a minute — just a sentence or two that tells people what you liked about *Valiant, He Endured*, to help other readers know why they might like it, too, and to help us write more of what you love.

The truth is, VERY FEW readers leave reviews.

Be the exception. Help us find our audience. Write a review today.

About the Editor

Former altar boy turned truancy fugitive, **George Donnelly** is an expat vagabond who prefers zombies to aliens but is primed for any meatspace apocalypse minus grey goo.

George discovered science fiction on July 4, 1980 at the Free Library of Philadelphia, Welsh Road Branch, when his dad got him an adult library card. Now a single dad with one son and two rescued cats, he's currently working on the next books in the Rork Sollix series.

EMAIL: me@georgedonnelly.com
WEBSITE: GeorgeDonnelly.com
FACEBOOK: AuthorGeorgeDonnelly
TWITTER: @GeorgeDonnelly

Also by George Donnelly

Rise the Renegade
Space pirate Rork Sollix's girl is made to pay for his crimes.

Human Free
A post-apocalyptic global warming novel free on WattPad.

Defiant, She Advanced
Book 1 in the *There Will be Liberty* anthology series.

Pink Slip Prophet
Robot cyberpunk with a sense of humor.